POLO
IN THE
ROUGH

Also by Jerry Kennealy

Polo's Ponies
Polo, Anyone?
Polo Solo

POLO
IN THE
ROUGH

Jerry Kennealy

ST. MARTIN'S PRESS
NEW YORK

Library of Congress Cataloging-in-Publication Data

Kennealy, Jerry.
     Polo in the rough : a Nick Polo mystery / Jerry
Kennealy.
          p.   cm.
     "A Thomas Dunne book."
     ISBN 0-312-02964-0
     I. Title.
PS3561.E4246P59 1989
813'.54—dc19   89-30131

First Edition

10 9 8 7 6 5 4 3 2 1

For my father, Frank.
It was a pleasure to know him,
a privilege to be his son.

POLO
IN THE
ROUGH

1

The cat scratched his way slowly across the car's hood, got a few inches from the windshield, and stared at me with that contemptuous look they get when you invade their territory. He was piebald and missing part of his right ear.

I stared back at him. We locked eyes for about ten seconds, then I stuck out my tongue at him and threw some popcorn out the car's window.

He gave me a Jack Nicholson grin and leaped off toward the popcorn. When he hit the ground, I saw he was limping.

I could understand the limp. He was now living in a tough neighborhood. Cute, quaint Carmel by the Sea. All those cozy little shops, art galleries, and jewelry stores are as cozy as ever, but when you get a few blocks away from the Snow White and the Seven Dwarfs cottages into where the locals actually live, you find out there is a little bit of trouble in paradise. It's not all champagne in a teacup anymore.

Rapes, daytime burglaries, even an occasional homicide, all the crimes that used to keep their place in the neighboring communities of Seaside, Pacific Grove, and Monterey have filtered into Carmel, and even Clint Eastwood hadn't been able to do much about it. The shutters are locked day and night, and the white-tailed squirrels have taken off and are being replaced by rats, big ones, that invade the gourmet garbage cans of the restaurants around Ocean Avenue. No wonder the cats traveled in packs of three and four. My God, we've got to take a stand. If we don't stop it here, what next? Pebble Beach? The mind boggles. Of course at six-twenty in the morning, my mind is about as boggled as it can get.

I was sitting uncomfortably in my rented sedan, with the standard stakeout kit: popcorn, a Thermos of coffee, and an empty mayonnaise jar, large mouth, for those untimely calls from mother nature.

I hate stakeouts. I simply don't have the patience, or the kidneys, for this kind of work anymore. But here I was waiting for Jack Slate, famous author, TV guest, and, according to one of my best clients, Attorney James Gilleran, the target of several recent death threats.

Slate had done a short stint with the U.S. State Department. His books—about the alleged conspiracies behind the deaths of Jack and Bobby Kennedy and the mob's involvement; the misdeeds of the CIA in the Middle East; the corruption in the Johnson and Nixon administrations; the blunders of the Reagan years—were all best-sellers. He had been on Larry King's television show a few days before and had made a few people nervous enough to call in death threats. The most nervous, though, was his publisher, who took the threats seriously and retained Jim Gilleran, who in turn hired me.

Gilleran told me that Slate usually spent his summers

at his house in Carmel. He was in town now for the golf tournament. Everyone still calls it the Crosby, though it's named after a corporate sponsor now. My job was to follow the author around during the day. I had to be discreet. Big, tough, Jack Slate was too macho to have a bodyguard, so I had to guard him, without him knowing it. Another poor soul took over at night. So, if things worked out, all I would have to do was slosh around Pebble Beach a few hours and have the evenings to myself. All in all, not a bad deal. Especially since I had intended to come down to watch the tournament anyway.

I measured out another cup of coffee and was surveying the area for a large tree that looked more appealing than the empty mayonnaise jar when a light went on in the second story of Slate's house. He was up a lot earlier than I thought he would be. The house was set back a little farther from the street than its neighbors. The walls were covered with umpteen coats of paint. The garden was neglected; overgrown privet hedges and rosebushes. A redwood fence, like a row of teeth in need of an orthodontist, strained against the weight of free-growing bottle brush shrubs. The place had the look of a home that was used a few weeks every year, then abandoned.

The downstairs lights went on a few minutes later. Another ten minutes went by and I heard a car's motor start up.

Slate pulled out from behind the privet hedge in a classic powder-blue Jaguar 1950s convertible with right-hand drive. The black canvas top was up, and as he passed by me I could see the car's paint was faded and the body riddled with dents. It sure looked like a real car, though.

I turned the rental around and followed him down

3

Dolores Street. He turned east on Ocean and up toward Highway 1.

The Jag, and the lack of traffic, made following a pleasure for a change. Following someone in a car is almost a bigger pain than a stakeout. To do it properly, you should have at least two cars, with radio controls. If the subject thinks he's being tailed, then you're going to need three or four vehicles, with two people in each car, so the subject can be followed by foot when he leaves his car. It gets expensive that way, which is why most tail jobs are done by one poor bastard with a nervous stomach. You just plant your nose close to your quarry's rear bumper and hope for the best. All that "stay back a few car lengths" stuff you hear on TV is just that. TV. You miss one red light in real life, and the sucker is gone.

There was no problem with Slate. The Jag took a right on Highway 1, then a left on Carmel Valley Road.

Traffic was starting to pick up a little bit, but it was still light. The sun was beginning to peep over the mountains. The sky was clear. The golfers would be happy. They'd be dry. Frozen maybe, but dry.

I wondered what Slate was doing up this early. The golf courses he was going to play in the tournament—Pebble Beach, Spyglass, and Cypress Point—were all back in the other direction. Maybe he was going to get in an early practice round at one of the outlying courses. He stayed on Carmel Valley Road for another few minutes, then turned off after a sign for Carmel Valley Airfield.

I coasted to a stop and watched as Slate got out of the Jag. He was shorter than I thought he would be, with a head full of tight gray curls. He was wearing jeans and a black leather jacket. He took a final sip from the coffee cup he was carrying, tossed the cup into the car, reached in and pulled out a camera with a long telephoto lens. He

4

slipped the camera's sling around his neck and walked over to a beige late-model Chevrolet. The driver of the Chevy got out, and they shook hands. He was a tall, thin guy, wearing a business suit. Their breath hit the cold air like smoke signals as they stood talking, then they walked over to a small, red-and-white single-engine plane. Slate climbed in the pilot's side, the other man into the passenger seat. The plane warmed up for a few minutes then took off. I watched it as it headed west, in the direction of the Pacific Ocean.

I pulled up next to Slate's car. He had left it unlocked. There was nothing inside other than the empty coffee mug. It smelled of whiskey. There was a small red sticker on the bottom left corner of the windshield that said "Participant Parking #535."

The other car was almost a duplicate of the one I was driving. The doors were locked. There was a rental form envelope from Avis on the front seat. I jotted down the license number in my notebook.

The airport wasn't much. A single runway of sand and dirt, with only an occasional patch of asphalt standing out from the weeds, pointed in a northwesterly direction. There were no runway lights. A red wind cone hung limply from a post. The only structure was a small concrete block building with a pay phone hanging from an outside wall. There were a total of eight single-engine planes, most of them looking in need of repair, scattered around the field.

I looked up into the brightening sky. There was no sign of Slate's airplane. There was no telling how long he would be gone. For all I knew he was flying down to Los Angeles, or Palm Springs. Or he could be back in ten minutes. At least it would give me time to replenish the coffee Thermos and use a real bathroom.

I doubled back down Carmel Valley Road, found a coffee shop, used the facilities, and got some coffee and a doughnut. There was a phone near the rest room. I looked up the local number for Avis.

"Hello, this is Sergeant Taylor, Monterey sheriff's office. We've got one of your cars that appears to have been in an accident and abandoned." I read off the license of the car at the airport.

The clerk checked through the records. She sounded a bit concerned when she came back on the line.

"Do you know where the driver is, Sergeant Taylor?" she asked.

"No. He may be out now looking for help."

"He should know how to find it," she said.

"How's that?"

"The car was rented to Thomas Dykstra, of the United States Secret Service."

2

I tried to digest the information, along with a glazed doughnut, as I drove back to the airstrip. The radio was playing a Tony Bennett record. Suddenly the announcer's voice cut in:

"We have just learned that a small airplane has crashed on Pebble Beach Golf Course. Preliminary reports from the scene indicate that there were two passengers. They have not been identified as yet. We will bring you further details as they develop. Now back to the program you were enjoying."

Bennett warbled back into "Just in Time." My stomach was feeling queasy, and I didn't necessarily think it was from the doughnut.

The Jaguar and the Chevrolet were parked in their same spots when I pulled back into the airstrip. There was no one else around. I sat and fiddled the radio dial, finally landing on an all-news station. They had an update on the crash. "Both occupants of the airplane were fatally injured. We do not know their identities yet. Our reporter will be on the scene shortly, and we will bring you details as they become available."

I turned the radio up as high as it would go, got out of the car, and went back to Slate's Jaguar. I rummaged around under the driver's seat and found the car keys. I unlocked the glove compartment and found nothing but an almost empty pint of Old Grand Dad. There were some crumbled papers, credit card receipts for gas, an old yellowing registration card. The trunk wasn't much bigger than the glove compartment and held nothing but some rusting hand tools.

I could hear the radio announcer interrupting a weather forecast.

"One of the two parties in the fatal plane crash at the Pebble Beach Golf Course has been identified as famed author Jack Slate. Mr. Slate was here to play in the AT&T Golf tournament and—"

I snapped the dial off and went to the pay phone on the small concrete block building's wall. James Gilleran answered on the sixth ring.

"Uhhh?" he said.

"It's me. Nick Polo. Problems."

"Shit. What the hell has that crazy man done? He can't be in trouble at this time of the morning," he said in a voice full of gravel.

"It's the last trouble he'll ever be in." I told Gilleran of the crash.

"God. I don't believe it. Do they know who the other victim was?"

"They may not yet, but I do. Slate drove down to the Carmel Valley airstrip this morning. A man was waiting for him. They took off together. I checked out the

8

guy's rental car. It was rented by a Thomas Dykstra of the United States Secret Service."

There was a long pause. "Shit," Gilleran finally said. "Hold on a minute, let me think about this."

It was more like three minutes. When he came back on the line he sounded in control.

"Okay, here's what I'd like you to do. Go back to his house. Get in somehow, I don't care how you do it. Start looking for a manuscript. Slate was supposed to be working on something hot, the publisher has been salivating over it. It's got to be there somewhere. We won't be needing that other investigator now. I'll call and cancel him."

Typical attorney. It's something they learn in law school. Never spend a nickel more on investigators than necessary.

"I imagine the police might be taking an interest in Slate's place pretty soon."

"Yeah," Gilleran said, "I know, but don't sweat it. Just tell them that you're working for me. I'll fix it somehow. If they lean on you, just have them call me."

"You have a lot more confidence in your influence with the police than I do, Gilleran."

"Nick, I know this is more than you bargained for, but do this for me. I'll take care of you, believe me."

The last time I had put all my faith in an attorney, it had cost me six months in jail.

Gilleran must have read my mind. "Nick, I'll handle it, believe me. We've got one of the biggest publishing houses in the world behind us. Trust me. Find that manuscript. I'll have the publisher's law department FAX me out power of attorney for Slate's property. I'm going to get dressed and come down there right now. I'll meet you at the house."

9

I drove back to Slate's place. It was as peaceful as when I left it.

The front door was locked and wedged tight. I went around the back, stepping over ankle-high weeds and rotting leaves. There was a pair of French windows leading into a back room. A simple hook latch was all that secured it. Slate must have been the trusting type. I popped the lock with a piece of celluloid I keep in my wallet for just such occasions. The first thing I noticed after I was inside was how warm it was. The thermostat must have been cranked up to eighty.

I was in a small office-library-den. There was an old pool table that had been converted into a desk. The top was littered with an electric typewriter, papers, books, envelopes, and old coffee cups and glasses.

I had to step around a half-dozen boxes stuffed with books. It looked like I was going to need the whole day just to go through this room.

I heard the screeching of brakes and knew I'd never have the time. They started ringing the bell, then pounding on the door.

I made my way to the front and opened the door. Two uniformed policemen stared back at me.

"Who are you?" the tallest one asked.

"It's a long story, officer," I said.

They took me to sheriff department headquarters on Aquajito Road and put me in a large empty room. The floor was green tiled linoleum. I'd like to know who the guy is that has the contract on that tile. He must be a very wealthy man. Every police station in the world seems to have the same damn stuff. There was a long table, surrounded by straight-backed wooden chairs, an old-fashioned water cooler, the kind with the upside-down bottle

10

of water and little plastic spout. There was a mirror that must have been six feet wide by four feet high against one wall. You don't think they'd stoop to having a two-way mirror, do you? I got up close to the mirror, took a book of matches from my pocket, and lit up. If it is a two-way mirror, and the lighting is right, you can sometimes see just who is peeking at you from the other side. Sometimes, but not this time. Either there wasn't enough fire-power from the match—the ideal instrument is a flashlight with a small, thin, powerful beam—or the damn thing was just a normal, everyday mirror.

I helped myself to a paper cup full of spring water and sat down and waited. It didn't take long. Two men, both in civilian clothes, burst into the room.

One looked like he was close to fifty, and too skinny to throw a shadow. He was wearing a crumpled blue suit that seemed at least a size too large. His hair was a graying brown and cut military style. The other was well over six feet tall, in his early forties, and had an aggressive, authoritative air about him. I pegged him for Secret Service or FBI.

He flapped an ID card at me and said, "Andrew Burke, Federal Bureau of Investigation. Sit down, Polo." Burke was wearing a dull-gray business suit, a white shirt with the collar so heavily starched it was already scoring a red line around his neck, gray tie, and heavily shined brogues. He was bald, except for some dark strands combed sideways, like pencil lines, across his scalp.

Burke pulled back the chair, dropped a briefcase on the table, and said, "Sit down, Polo," again.

I turned to the other guy. "Who are you?"

"Lieutenant Shroyer, Monterey County Sheriff." He took his suit coat off and draped it over the back of a

11

chair. There were sweat marks under the arms of his wrinkled blue shirt.

"Polo," Burke said, "I want to help you, but you must understand that you're in serious trouble. I think it would be best if you gave us a detailed statement right now."

"Can I ask a question?" I said.

Burke's head nodded up and down. "Certainly."

"Just what am I doing here?"

"What are you doing here? You were caught in the middle of a burglary. You're an ex-con. The home you broke into belonged to a man who has just been killed. That's what the hell you're doing here."

"I didn't break into the house. I'm a licensed private investigator. The door was unlocked. I was advised to enter the premises by Mr. Slate's attorney."

"And who might that be?" asked Shroyer.

"James P. Gilleran."

Burke's basilisk eyes were swiveling between Shroyer and me.

"Who's this Gilleran?" he asked.

"San Francisco attorney," Shroyer said. "I've heard of him."

"What the hell would Slate be doing with a Frisco attorney?" asked Burke. "And just when did he advise you to break into Slate's house?"

"I called him when I heard about the plane crash. Gilleran was hired by Slate's publisher to take care of Slate while he was in Carmel."

Shroyer said, "And you're working for Slate as what? A bodyguard?"

"More of a discreet chaperon, I think you'd say."

Shroyer went to the water cooler. "So you were following Slate? Since when?"

12

"Since early this morning."

"Where did you follow him?" Burke piped in.

"He left his house before seven. Drove directly to the Carmel Valley Airfield. Met a guy there. They flew off, that's it. I heard about the crash on the radio and called Mr. Gilleran."

Burke stood up. "Lieutenant, I have an agent at the Monterey Peninsula Airport. You should send someone out to the—"

Shroyer waved him down with his hand. "Already taken care of." He turned his attention back to me. "Did you get a good look at the man Slate met?"

"Yes. White, middle-aged, wearing a suit and tie."

"Ever see him before?"

"Never."

"Was there anyone else at the airport?"

"Just Slate and the other man."

"Did you notice the other man's car?"

"Yes. Late-model Chevrolet. They seemed to know each other. They shook hands, spoke for a couple of minutes, then got into the airplane. Slate was the pilot."

Shroyer moved close to me. His eyes were almost the same shade of blue as his shirt. He had more than his share of crow's feet. I wondered if they were the result of smiling or of frowning too much.

"What did the plane do after it took off?" he asked.

"Flew west, out toward the ocean."

"You didn't see it turn north or south?"

"Nope. After it took off, I went and picked up some coffee and a doughnut. I heard about the crash on the radio. Then I called Gilleran."

"I think we should hold him until the Secret Service people get here, Lieutenant," said Burke.

I stood up and looked Burke in the eye. "I'd like to

13

cooperate with you gentlemen, but if you're going to start talking about holding me, then either specify the charges or I walk out of here right now. You want any further information, you'll have to clear it with Gilleran."

Burke climbed out of his chair and came over and stuck a chubby finger into my chest. "We know all about you, Polo. You spent some time in a federal prison. If you don't cooperate, you'll be spending a lot more time in one." He went back to sticking his finger in my chest. "That's"—finger—"a"—finger—"promise"—finger.

Federal authorities can be a real pain in the ass when they're acting polite. When they come on strong, they're impossible. Burke looked like he flunked the polite class at the FBI academy.

"I bruise easy, Burke, so stick your finger where it will do some good." I turned to Shroyer. "Lieutenant, are there any other questions?"

He ran a hand across his jaw. "When does Gilleran get in?"

"He said he was leaving right after I called him this morning. It's only a two-hour drive. He should be in soon."

"Where are you meeting him?"

"Slate's place."

He nodded his head. "Okay. Why don't we all go and wait for him?"

3

Gilleran arrived in style, in the backseat of a luminously shining dark-blue stretch Cadillac limousine. His chauffeur, Max, a tall, broad-shouldered man with balloons of scar tissue over his eyes, opened the back door for him.

Gilleran spotted me first and walked over and extended a hand. He was wearing his usual going-to-court suit, a well-tailored blue pinstripe. I know he flies to England a couple of times a year just to get his suits made. He wore a light-gray shirt and a silk tie, just a half shade darker than the shirt. A red handkerchief flowered out of his suit jacket pocket. The look was expensive, and perhaps a little overdone, a little "foppish," as the English like to say. But his face was all business: craggy with hard-work lines. The nose had been broken by a wayward fist years ago. A shock of gray hair flopped boyishly over his broad forehead.

I introduced him to Lieutenant Shroyer and Andrew Burke.

15

"Look here," Burke said in an officious tone, "We caught your man here breaking in and—"

"I don't believe you could call what Mr. Polo did breaking in, sir," Gilleran said, his voice soft and eminently reasonable. He took some papers from an alligator-skin briefcase and handed them to Burke. "Since Mr. Polo is my agent, and we represent Mr. Slate and his estate, Mr. Polo had every right to enter the house on my instructions."

Burke snatched the papers from Gilleran's hand. "I'm afraid that under these circumstances . . ."

Gilleran put on his courtroom voice. "Under these circumstances, Mr. Burke, we are stuck with each other. I want to cooperate with the authorities in every possible way, but I also have an obligation to my client. You must realize that Mr. Slate was a very famous man. He has some papers in his home that are quite valuable to his publisher and his estate. I'm here to protect their interests. If there are any documents that in any way relate to Mr. Slate's death, rest assured that I will supply them to you. I will also instruct Mr. Polo to cooperate fully with you. Quite frankly, I don't understand just what interest the Federal Bureau of Investigation has in this incident."

Shroyer was leaning against the fender of his car, taking it all in, a toothpick dangling from his lips.

"You mean your boy Polo here didn't tell you about who was in the plane with Slate?" Shroyer asked.

"No. And there hasn't been an announcement of any kind on the radio. Who was the passenger?" Gilleran asked with a straight face.

"Ask Polo," Shroyer said.

I shrugged my shoulders. "Beats me."

Shroyer dropped his toothpick to the dirt and ground it out under his heel as if it were a cigarette. "You surprise

16

me, Polo. A sharpie like you, why didn't *you* ask why the hell the FBI was sticking its nose into a local airplane accident."

"I guess I thought the local police needed outside help."

That got me a nasty smile from Shroyer. He put another toothpick between his teeth. "When we found Dykstra's rental car at the airport, I checked with Avis. Some sharpie called into Avis this morning, told them that he was with the Monterey sheriff's office. Told them that this certain car was in an accident. The Avis clerk checked for him and told him the car was rented to a Secret Service agent."

Burke's pink complexion was getting redder by the second.

"Why don't we go inside and discuss this like gentlemen?" Gilleran said, holding out his arm like an usher pointing to the loges.

Burke gave him a nasty look, then waved for Shroyer to follow him.

Gilleran walked over to me. "Were you able to find the manuscript?"

"No, the cops got here right after I did."

He looked around at the cars. In addition to Shroyer's unmarked sedan, there was a van marked "Monterey County Sheriff Crime Lab."

"Nick, can you check to see if the house has been bugged?"

"I can look, but I don't have the right tools, and I'm not really an expert."

He nodded his head, keeping an eye on Burke, who was standing in the front doorway waiting for him.

"Get someone. Today if possible. I don't trust these

17

bastards. Once they leave, we've got to turn the place up-side down to find that damn manuscript."

I walked the six blocks toward the center of Carmel and found a little restaurant fixed up like a Swiss chalet. I used the pay phone to call John Henning, a San Francisco private investigator who is an electronics wizard. He wasn't working on anything that wouldn't keep for a cou-ple of days, so he agreed to meet me at Slate's house later in the afternoon. I bought a newspaper and took my time over a cheese omelet and fresh scones.

There were a few more cars parked around Slate's place when I got back. I brought a cup of coffee in a Styrofoam cup over to Gilleran's chauffeur.

"Getting crowded around here," I said, handing him the cup through the car's window.

"Yeah. I think the district attorney was called in. Might be a while. Hop in."

I got in the front seat and we shot the breeze about the 49ers and horse racing for half an hour, then I took a short nap. Max woke me up when Gilleran came to the front door, surrounded by Shroyer, Burke, and two ner-vous-looking, middle-aged men in business suits. They shook hands, then left, followed almost immediately by three guys in neat coveralls, carrying boxes and canvas bags.

I waited until everyone had gone, then got out and went over to Gilleran.

He walked out toward the car. "The first thing we do is find that damn manuscript," he said. "We can look all we want, but we can't take anything out of the house. That's the agreement, but if we find that manuscript, all bets are off. Fuck 'em, we can always say that Slate mailed the damn thing in, or something." He took off his suit coat and rolled up his sleeves and walked back to the front door. "Let's get started."

18

The house seemed somehow larger from inside. A long entrance hall, the parquet floor scratched bare in places where it wasn't covered by a rug. The traces from the police lab experts were visible: upholstered sofa and chairs with cushions askew, fine powder on top of traditional cherrywood furniture. There were several paintings lying against the walls; pale, dusty spots on the fading beige walls showed where they had originally hung.

"Let's start in the office," Gilleran said, as he stalked off down the hallway.

He opened the drapes and what sunshine there was streamed in through the French windows.

We worked for a good hour, sorting through the desk and cardboard cartons on the floor.

The only thing of interest I found was a heavily embossed envelope addressed to Slate at an address in Palm Springs. It was the invitation to play in the golf tournament. There was a list of the amateurs and their professional partners, a blue ribbon with the instructions for wearing it to identify yourself as a participant in the tournament, and an invitation to the big clambake party on Wednesday night.

Gilleran straightened up and dusted off his hands. "I'm getting hungry. I'll send Max for something to eat."

"Good idea. I'll take a quick check of the rest of the place."

A staircase near the front door led to the upper floor, which consisted of two bedrooms and two baths. One of the bedrooms was a mishmash of tangled clothes and bed sheets. There was a half-empty glass with a lipstick smear near the bed. I sniffed the glass. Gin. There was a pair of red silk women's slacks on the floor. I picked them up. Size 8. The label was Gucci. The closet was a mixture of men's and women's clothing: suits, jackets, blouses, skirts.

19

There was an old shotgun leaning against the back of the closet. I picked it up. A Purdy double-barrel .12 gauge with exposed hammers and individual triggers. The stock was bird's-eye maple but, like the engraved barrel, was badly scratched. I broke open the breech. It was loaded. I extracted the cartridges, put them in my pocket, and laid the shotgun back to rest.

The other room was neater, the closet empty. A guest room that seldom saw a guest.

I went back downstairs. Gilleran was in the kitchen, trying to figure out how to get the coffee machine to work. The floor was a bright-yellow linoleum, and sticky from spilled drinks. Copper pots and cooking utensils hung over a tiled gas stove. A big almond-color double-door freezer-refrigerator stood next to the stove. I opened the refrigerator door. There were several bottles of champagne, Mumm's, some white wines, two six-packs of Guinness beer, tubes of ready-to-bake biscuits, bacon, a carton of eggs and some unopened cellophane-wrapped pieces of cheddar cheese, and a tub of cottage cheese. The expiration date on the cottage cheese was over a week away, so apparently Slate had bought most of his groceries recently.

I took out two of the beers, found an opener in a drawer, and brought them over to Gilleran.

"Here, this will save you the trouble of figuring out how that coffeepot works."

He took a swig from the bottle. "I've got to get back to the city, Nick. If we don't find that manuscript today, I'd like you to stick around and look for it. Where are you staying?"

"I've got a reservation at the Holiday Inn in Monterey."

"Cancel it, move in here. It'll save us the expense of hiring a security guard."

"There are some women's clothes upstairs. Apparently Slate had company," I said.

"I'd like to find her. Maybe she knows something about the manuscript. Maybe she'll be coming back for her clothes."

"Tell me about Slate," I said.

Gilleran ran the cold bottle of beer across his forehead. "Interesting guy. Married and divorced four times. His parents were wealthy. He went to work for the State Department for a while. Wrote his first book exposing a lot of the boys on Foggy Bottom. Quit. Just kept on writing. Made a lot of money from his books. He liked writing, drinking, women, and golf, though not necessarily in that order. He came across as a liberal intellectual, but from what I heard from his New York lawyer, he's got a portfolio worthy of a conservative Boston banker. There's going to be a real free-for-all over his estate. All those ex-wives."

"Any kids?"

"Nope. Not that we know of, but I'm sure there will be several hopeful heirs to the throne popping out of the woodwork." He took a sip of the beer. "I'd give a lot to know just what he was doing this morning with that Secret Service agent. So would Burke."

Max came in with a box of delicatessen goodies that made me sorry I had overdone the omelet and scones.

After they ate we went back to the library. There was no sign of the manuscript Gilleran was looking for.

"Just what's so special about this manuscript anyway?" I asked.

"Special? Well, anything that Slate wrote is bound to be a big seller, no matter if it was good or not. But he was all jacked up about this one. It had to do with the Shah of Iran and the money taken out of the country when he took off."

21

"Shah of Iran? Isn't that old news?"

Gilleran gave me a quick, probing look. "Old news? You still read about caches of Nazi gold and valuable paintings rotting away in some vault, or the tons of gold that the Japanese were supposed to have buried in the Philippines. That's old news, but it keeps popping up. Even if it were true, it would be small stuff compared to what they whisked out of Iran. In his prime, the shah was taking in twenty-two billion dollars a year in oil revenues. That's billion, not million. And the good old U.S. of A. was kicking in some five hundred million for military aid. There's no telling how many Swiss banks had to add on extra rooms of safety-deposit boxes to keep the stuff from mildewing. No, not old news, Nick, just news that never got much publicity." He reached for the phone and punched out half a phone number, then put the receiver back on its cradle. "Were you able to get anyone to check out that problem I asked you about?"

I nodded. "It will be taken care of."

He rolled down his sleeves and reached for his suit jacket. "Good, come on, Max. Let's get out of here."

4

After Gilleran left, I took my suitcase out of the trunk of the rental car, put it in the spare bedroom upstairs, then puttered around looking for the manuscript. There was a separate garage, just about big enough to hold the little Jaguar. Nothing there except two old tires, some oil spots on the floor, and Slate's golf clubs. The golf bag was of imitation black leather. I picked up one of the irons. There were bits of grass and dirt in the grooves. I dug through the bag, finding a windbreaker and rain pants jammed in one zippered pocket and balls, tees, and golf gloves in another.

I went back up to the bedroom and straightened it up, wondering about the woman. There was nothing there at all to say who she was; no pictures, address books, not even any monograms on her clothes. I went through Slate's clothes, pocket by pocket, and found nothing other than some change, golf tees, and soiled handkerchiefs.

John Henning arrived a little after four o'clock. Henning's a lanky, rawboned man getting close to sixty. I had done him a few small favors when I was in the police department and, after I left the department and had gone through a small inheritance in record time, thanks to a stockbroker who introduced me to the wonderful world of options, I opened up shop as a private investigator. I would have either starved or gone into another line of work if John hadn't shown me the difference between police work and being a private investigator. His specialty was electronics.

Electronics are really simple enough. You can buy anything from a basic telephone transmitter to the latest in infrared audio monitoring gadgets. You can buy them, but they're expensive as hell. Henning can walk into the nearest Radio Shack, pick up a harmless-looking collection of couplers, transistors, microbatteries, and God knows what else for about ten bucks, and build a bug that the CIA would drool over.

He was carrying a battered old fishing tackle box. He pulled out something from the box that looked like a curling iron and went to work. In less than an hour he had performed a full security sweep on the house and garage.

"Nothing there now, Nick," he said.

"Now? Does that mean there was something?"

"Yep. Unless the crime lab was awful sloppy. Come over here."

He turned the phone on Slate's desk upside down and undid the bottom plate.

"Here," he said, handing me a magnifying glass and placing a bony finger alongside the screws that held a set of red, yellow, black, and green wires.

I looked through the glass. "Uh-huh," I mumbled as if I actually spotted something.

24

"See the screw slots? They've been used since the phone company manufactured that baby. And whoever did it didn't have the right size screwdriver."

"Uh-huh," I said again, a little louder, now that I actually could see what he meant. The slots on the screws were definitely gouged out of shape.

"So what type bug do you think they were using?"

Henning put the phone back together. "Hard to tell. Depends on who set it up. Some kind of simple battery-operated transmitter, I would guess. But that's just a guess."

"But there aren't any bugs in the house now."

"Nope. I can guarantee that. Not one."

"Okay. I'd like the house bugged now. This room, the kitchen, living room, the upstairs bedrooms. Can you do that?"

"That depends," Henning said, his head bobbing up and down on his thin neck.

"Money isn't a problem, John."

"I wasn't worried about the money, Nick. I just hope there's a Radio Shack nearby. I didn't bring a whole lot of equipment with me."

Henning found his Radio Shack and did a simple hard-wired bugging job, using the phones in the kitchen, den, and upstairs bedrooms, and a self-concocted transmitter in the living and dining rooms. Each bug was hooked up to a separate VOX, voice-activated micro-cassette recorder that would automatically turn itself on at the first sound.

It was well past eight o'clock when he was finished. I invited him to stay for dinner, but he said he was in a hurry to get back home. John has been an on-and-off member of Alcoholics Anonymous for years. I've gotten

25

the feeling that he thinks I feel uncomfortable drinking in front of him. He's probably right.

After he left, I helped myself to the wine in the refrigerator and had a dinner of the leftovers from lunch: chicken, pâté, potato salad, cheese cake. Max knew how to shop. While we had been looking for the manuscript, he had made himself useful by straightening up the kitchen, so now everything looked reasonably clean.

I had the TV on during dinner. Slate's plane crash was still the big news of the day.

They had finally released the information about Secret Service agent Thomas Dykstra being in the plane with Slate. He was described as "a veteran officer currently on leave and, according to government sources, was getting ready to retire from the service." The other big news was that "informed sources" had stated that the cause of the crash could have been due to a bomb on board the plane.

I had figured on the possibility of the woman coming back. Now I was worried that someone else might drop by. Was one lousy manuscript worth all of that trouble?

I sat in the front room. A cold wind was prying at the windows, rattling the glass, searching for an entry. I thought about turning on the furnace, or dumping a log or two into the flagstone fireplace, but I settled for one of Slate's sweaters under my sport coat and some of his cognac, Delamain Très Venerable, a brand I'd never heard of. Judging from the taste, even if I had heard of it, I wouldn't have been able to afford it.

I sat there, yawning, wondering if I was wasting my time. If someone was watching the house, they'd know I was here. But maybe all the traffic, with Gilleran and his chauffeur, Shroyer and Burke's men, and John Henning's coming and going would have confused anyone who had an urge to come in for a look. Besides, surveillance on the house would be difficult now. There was always the possibility of the police making a passing call.

The ringing phone shattered the silence. It went on for twelve rings, stopped, then started up again. This time for thirteen rings. I drained what was left of the cognac, set the balloon snifter down, took a .25 Beretta out of its ankle holster and put it in my pocket. Slate's shotgun was lying on the floor next to my feet. I picked it up, loaded it, and laid it across my lap. I checked my watch. The night had turned into morning.

It was about fifteen minutes later when I heard the first sound: a soft, raspy noise. From the back of the house. Slate's den. I waited until I heard a louder noise. Footsteps? I got up slowly, taking one cautious step at a time, the shotgun snuggled in my arms.

If someone was going to break in, Slate's office certainly was the ideal choice: in the back, out of sight of the neighbors, ground level, no windowsill to climb over, just those French windows, which, as I had found out, were ridiculously simple to open. A streak of light showed from the door to the den, then disappeared quickly.

The noises were getting louder now, as if the intruder was gaining confidence with every passing second. I could make out the sound of drawers being opened, papers rifled. I closed my eyes and strained my ears. How many were there? It sounded like just one person. Would there be a backup waiting in a car outside? I backed away toward the front door, so I could get outside quickly if I had to.

The den's door opened suddenly. There was silence, then the beam of a flashlight came into view, followed by a tall, darkly clothed figure. The light beam waved back

27

and forth, as if deciding which way to go. It finally started down the hall, toward the living room.

I was well hidden behind a large walnut armoire. The light came my way. I could hear the intruder's quick, nervous breaths as he walked by. I waited until he was just past me, then lashed out a foot, aiming toward his knees. As he was falling I brought the barrel of the shotgun down in a short arc toward his head. There was a sickening sound of metal meeting flesh and bone as he crumpled to the ground, the flashlight bouncing down the hall. I picked up the flashlight and found the light switch. The sudden burst of light blinded me momentarily. I blinked my eyes rapidly. The man on the floor was lying still. I switched off the lights and counted slowly to a hundred. The only sounds were from the wind. I put the lights back on and knelt down next to the guy on the floor, keeping the barrel of the shotgun jammed into his neck. I frisked him quickly with one hand, finding an automatic in a brand-new, stiff leather holster under his arm. I stuck the pistol in my waistband. He was groaning now. I grabbed him by his lank hair and banged his head against the floor.

"Just stay still," I said. "I'll tell you when to talk."

There was no resistance as I went through his pockets, coming out with a cheap leather wallet, a ring of keys, a pocket knife, and a dirty gray handkerchief. I stood up and backed off a few feet and went through the wallet. The wallet's plastic identification holder displayed a green card from the Bureau of Collections and Investigations, showing that Paul Sanders was a licensed private investigator. I checked the ID picture on his PI license and his driver's license with the face on the floor. The hair was shorter in the pictures, but it was the same man: thick lips, protruding eyes shadowed by heavy eyebrows and a nose that was flatter than the one he was born with. Sanders's driver's license showed him with a Monterey address, height six foot one, weight two hundred and forty pounds, age twenty-eight. He was wearing a black raincoat and gloves.

"Stand up, Sanders."

He wobbled to his feet, massaging his neck with one hand. "You're in a lot of trouble, buddy," he said in a strained, hoarse voice.

"Am I now? And what about you? Breaking and entering, carrying a concealed weapon."

"I've got a permit for the gun, buddy. I'm a cop, and—"

"No. You haven't got a permit. The only things in your wallet are your licenses, four fifty-dollar bills, a few ones, a receipt from a sporting goods store for a holster you bought earlier today, and a picture of a nice-looking blonde in a bikini. You're not a cop, just a private eye, which carries no weight at all. I can have your license suspended for just carrying this cannon."

He was bouncing back and forth from one foot to the other, as if he had to go to the bathroom. His eyes were narrowing, he seemed to be measuring the distance between us. I pushed the shotgun toward him and told him to turn around, and when he did I kicked him in the back of his right knee. He fell to the floor again.

"You're not very bright, Sanders. You were thinking of jumping me, weren't you?"

He stared up at me with hate-filled eyes. "You'll be sorry for that, buddy. I—"

"You call me buddy one more time and I'm going to break that leg." I cradled the shotgun in my arms and examined his gun, a new-looking .45 Colt Commander. Too much gun for Sanders. Too much gun for anyone, really. I pulled back the slide and found that the chamber was loaded. I ejected the bullets one by one. They made small clinking sounds as they hit the floor.

"Want to tell me why you're here, or do I just call the cops?" I asked him.

Sanders coughed, trying to clear his throat. "I got a right to be here. The owner gave me permission. You're the one who's in shit."

"The owner gave you permission? That's interesting. When was this?"

"That's my business."

I tapped his leg with the shotgun. "Do you want to walk around with a limp for the rest of your life, Sanders? I can shoot you, break a few bones, then call the cops and I'll still be the good guy. You'll be in the hospital, without a license and looking forward to a few years in prison." I pushed the twin barrels of the shotgun into his groin and pulled back both hammers. "Now! What the hell are you doing here?"

"Easy, buddy, easy, take it easy," he said, his voice veering up and down the scale. "The guy that owns this place hired me. Said his wife kicked him out. He just wanted to see what was going on. Said she was away and he had some . . . stuff he wanted." He held out his arms helplessly. "Hell, it's his house."

"This fellow give you a name?"

"Yes, Wilson. Joe Wilson."

"If this is his house, why didn't he just give you the key?"

"He said his wife had the locks changed." Sanders smiled, showing a lot of pink gum over small gray teeth. "Getting in was a piece of cake."

"Getting out might be more of a problem. Did this Wilson give you a check?"

"No. Cash. Three hundred bucks."

"Where does Wilson live?"

"He's staying at some motel in Carmel."

I shook my head. "Pays cash. No local address, gives you a story about the ex-wife, and you go out and play commando for three hundred dollars. How long have you been in this business, Sanders?"

"On my own? Just a few months."

"What was it that this Wilson wanted you to pick up?"

Sanders's forehead serrated with wrinkles. "That's confidential. Say, who are you, anyway?"

"I'm the man with the shotgun, and you're the guy on the floor. What did he want?"

"If I tell you everything, what happens to me?"

"You walk out of here."

Sanders wiped his lips on the back of his gloved hand. "Okay. This Wilson is some kind of a writer. He had a book he was working on. His old lady was holding it back on him, pushing for more dough. He wanted me to find the book and check the house out. See who his wife was shacking up with."

"And you believed all of that?"

He wiped the back of his hand across his mouth, as if wiping away a bad taste. "I believed the three hundred balloons."

I tossed him his wallet and ordered him back into the den. "Get behind the desk. Can you type?"

"Sure, but . . ."

"What does Wilson look like?"

"Tall, well built. Dark hair. Maybe a little faggy."

"Type just what I tell you."

He started to protest and I popped him lightly on the top of his head with the shotgun.

31

Sanders took off his gloves, threaded a piece of paper into Slate's machine, and began typing. His clumsy two-finger style took some time and we went through three drafts before I was satisfied.

"Now sign it. And if you give me any trouble, I'll turn this letter, and your gun, over to the local police. Meanwhile, use what little intelligence you have to try and run down this Wilson. When you find him, don't talk to him, just call me." I took out one of my business cards. "Write your phone number on the back of the card."

Sanders studied the card for a moment, then screamed. "Shit, you're just a private eye!" He burst out of the chair, his right hand balling into a fist.

I clipped him on the head with the shotgun's stock, then kicked at his leg, then brought my knee up into his face. He let out a sound like bathwater draining out of the tub, then dropped to the floor.

I heard a car's racing motor, the crunching of tires over gravel. I raced toward the front door. Whoever it was, wasn't trying to be sneaky. Sanders's backup must have gotten impatient.

The door opened suddenly and a tall, dark-haired young woman in a bright-yellow raincoat came into the house.

"Who the hell are you?" she asked.

I gestured with the shotgun. "Come in. Close the door behind you."

She seemed to consider the request for a moment, then turned and slammed the door shut.

"I hope you know what you're doing," she said as she spun back to face me. Her eyes were dark, doe shaped, and showed no fear at all.

"Toss your purse over here, and take off that coat."

She flung the purse hard enough to make me wince as I caught it with one hand.

"I'm afraid you're going to be disappointed," she said, unbuttoning the coat. "There's very little money in there, and if you think I'm going to take off anything more than this coat without a struggle, you're sadly mistaken."

I fingered through the purse, which was a small, maroon leather job with the distinctive Gucci clasp.

"What did you come back for, your clothes?"

She tossed her raincoat on the ground in a defiant gesture and stood, feet slightly apart, arms on her hips.

"Fuck you" was all that she would say.

She looked to be in her mid- to late-twenties, and she looked vaguely familiar. She was dressed all in black, sweater, slacks, boots. Her hair was so dark it had a hint of blue in it. She hadn't lied about her wallet. A lone twenty-dollar bill, a few coins, an American Express card, a Visa, and a New York driver's license. They all showed the same name. Vanilla Hale.

"Vanilla?" I asked skeptically.

"My father had two passions. Ice cream was one of them."

There was a loud banging noise, then the crashing of glass.

The girl folded her arms across her chest. "Friends of yours?"

"Another uninvited guest," I said, shepherding her down the hallway. Paul Sanders had taken off in a hurry. The French windows were wide open.

"No one seems to want to be in your company, Mr. . . . whoever you are. That includes me. If you'd just put away Jack's shotgun, I'll pack my bags and be on my way."

I lowered the Purdy. "Where have you been, Miss Hale?"

"None of your fucking business."

33

"I think fucking is more in your line of work, lady.. My name is Nick Polo. I'm working for an attorney representing Slate's estate. This house is part of that estate. We wouldn't want anyone walking out with something that didn't belong to them."

There was a cold silence of thirty seconds, then her lower lip curled a little. "This isn't going very well, is it?" She shivered lightly. "It's cold in here. Any reason we can't have a little heat?"

"None that I can think of."

She obviously knew her way around the house. She went right to the thermostat, sidestepping Sanders's bullets scattered along the floor, then walked into the front room.

"Let's split the chores," she said. "One of us starts the fire, the other fixes the drinks."

"I'm a city boy, I'll get the drinks."

I poured two hefty measures of Slate's cognac into fresh glasses, while she expertly arranged rolled newspapers, small kindling sticks, and logs in the fireplace.

She smiled up at me from her kneeling position on the stone hearth. "Matches?"

I handed her a pack from the coffee table.

"There. That's better," she said, once the papers caught on fire. She cocked her head to one side. "You don't look like a rent-a-cop."

"Tell me about you and Slate."

She perched on the edge of the hearth and sipped her drink with small, dainty swallowing sounds, then licked her lips. "Jack and I were together the last few months on a more or less permanent basis. No strings attached. We . . . enjoyed each other's company."

"When did you get to Carmel?"

"About a week ago. Jack was all excited about this

34

boring golf tournament. He had played in the Bob Hope tournament in Palm Springs a couple of weeks ago, went to L.A. to do some TV shows. Then we flew up here."

"Was he doing any writing?"

She combed her hair with her fingers. "Always. He'd write things down all the time. Anywhere. Everywhere. In cabs, restaurants, on the back of matchbooks, theater programs, menus, anything."

From the fireplace came a series of cracks, a bright moment of flame, and the smell of sap as the kindling caught fire.

"What about serious writing?" I asked. "I understand he was working on a book."

"I think he was working on three or four projects. He was always busy."

"I'm interested in a recent manuscript he was working on. About the Shah of Iran."

She tilted the snifter back, then asked, "Any more of this stuff in the bottle?"

I topped off her glass. The fire was going good now, the room warming up rapidly.

"I know Jack was working on something about the shah, but I don't know the details. I think he finished it."

"Where would the manuscript be?"

"Somewhere around here. His office, I guess. Unless he wrapped it up and sent it to his publisher. Or maybe he had it on the plane with him."

"Why was Slate flying that early in the morning? And with a Secret Service agent. Did you know Dykstra?"

"I don't remember ever hearing the name. Jack loved to fly. He used to own his own planes, then found out it was cheaper to rent them."

"You're lucky you weren't in the air with him this time."

She stood up, holding her hands out to the now-roaring fire. "I'm not likely to be up at that time of the morning. Besides, Jack and I were sort of winding things down. I don't think it would have lasted much longer. We were both getting a little restless, and I can't stand this cold weather. That's why I was in Palm Springs, soaking up the sun, when I heard the news."

She held her hands up to the fire. "Ummm, that feels good. I love the heat." She arched her back, pushing her breasts upward. She caught my eyes and smiled.

"I'd like you to help me look for that manuscript," I said.

She pulled up the bottom of her sweater and began rubbing her index finger around her belly button. "Can't that wait until morning?" she said. Her voice was either getting awfully husky or my ears were fogging up.

"Yes, it can wait."

She laughed. She had me on her sexual hook and knew it.

"I'm worried about your friend who busted out the back windows," she said. "What if he comes back?"

"We'll just have to be careful."

"Yes, that's one thing we'll have to be, all right."

She turned her back to me and pulled her sweater off and stretched her arms out to the fire again. She wasn't wearing a bra.

I stood there staring at that beautiful back, knowing that it was all too easy. Much too easy. I was in Slate's house, eating his food, drinking his liquor, and now his girl was coming onto me with a seductiveness that bordered on rape. Too easy. She turned around, her eyes all-knowing, her tongue darting out to lick her lips. The heat from the fire had started her perspiring. I watched a drop of sweat trickle down her chest, between her magnificent

36

breasts. It seemed to hang there a minute, then continued its way down toward her stomach. Her mouth tasted of the brandy and she kissed me so hard I could feel her teeth. Too easy, I kept thinking as we entwined ourselves and slowly sank to the carpet. But life is hard, then you die. Why fight the easy times?

5

You couldn't exactly call it "lovemaking," or any similar romantic term. It was more of a sexual battle. We ripped off the rest of each other's clothes, grabbed and clutched at our bodies, and rolled around on the rug. At one point she straddled me and I could see our shadows cast on the wall and ceiling by the light from the fireplace. Her head was thrown back, her breasts swirling as she thrusted violently up and down, swearing and mumbling words I couldn't understand. If the Marquis De Sade was there he would have been clapping enthusiastically with one hand.

She climaxed in long, thigh-tightening shudders, and I followed right behind her, out of ecstasy or relief or fear.

She picked up her clothes and padded off upstairs without saying a word.

I checked myself for any missing parts, then got my clothes, poured a much-needed shot of brandy, picked up all the armament, the Beretta, Sanders's .45, and the shotgun, and, in a classic case of doing the right thing a little late, checked the downstairs doors and windows, including the one Sanders had broken in and out of. The whole Russian army could have marched through the living room ten minutes ago, and I wouldn't have even noticed them.

There was little possibility that Lieutenant Shroyer would be working at this time of the morning, which was fine with me. I called the Monterey sheriff's department, asked for him, was told he wouldn't be in until morning, then left my name. Now when he got all hot and bothered about not being notified that Slate's girlfriend had shown up, I could tell him in all honesty that I tried to get hold of him.

I went upstairs. The door to Slate's bedroom was closed. I reached out for it, then pulled my hand back and went into the guest room. The sheets were new, crisp, and cold. I was asleep seconds after my head hit the pillows.

The sound of the door opening woke me, and my hand groped to the nightstand for the Beretta. Vanilla stood in the doorway; she was still naked. She strode over and climbed in beside me. This time it was lovemaking: soft, careful, tender, delicious. No swearing or grunting. She snuggled up under my arm, her head on my chest, then fell asleep.

When I woke up she was gone. I panicked, tripping as I got out of bed, and hastily put on pants and a shirt. If she took off now, she'd be hell to catch. But she was in Slate's study flipping through the pages of the books on the wall, dressed in her black sweater and black pants outfit.

"Find anything interesting?" I asked.

She turned quickly and I saw a brief moment of fear

39

in those doe eyes. They hardened quickly. "No, not really." She dropped the book to the floor, selected another one, and began flipping through it.

"How about you or the police?" she asked.

"If they found anything, they didn't tell me, and so far I've drawn a blank as far as his manuscript. What were you looking for?"

"Oh, just notes. Jack would often be reading a book, then get an idea, and jot something down on a scrap of paper, or right in the book."

"What were his interests? Other than his writing."

She gave a nervous brush to the hair that had fallen over her forehead. "The usual, I guess. Power, money, success, sex. Having bigger and better toys than all the other boys."

I picked up the book she had dropped to the floor, *The Trivia Encyclopedia*.

"That was another of Jack's interests. Trivia. He would know the damnedest, stupidest things. Anything about movies, TV, the comics. He was like a little kid. He liked to play at being a private eye or a secret agent. When he was doing background on a book, he'd use all these crazy names. One time he was Miles Archer."

"Sam Spade's partner," I said.

She smiled. "That's right. Then he was Felix Leiter."

I drew a blank on that one.

"Leiter was James Bond's buddy at the CIA. Jack loved playing little games with people like that. He enjoyed putting people down, making them look foolish."

"I wonder what *nom de plume* he was using last?" I said.

"I don't know. It could be anything."

"Getting hungry?" I asked.

40

"I'm afraid you're going to be very disappointed if you ask me to cook."

"You start the coffee," I said. "I'll handle the cooking."

I made it simple, bacon, eggs, and toast. I wolfed my food down, while she pushed hers around her plate, rearranging it rather than actually eating.

"I guess you just weren't hungry," I said, wiping egg yolk from my lips with a paper napkin.

"I never was much for breakfast," she said, getting up to pour us more coffee.

The phone shrilled. I answered it. It was Shroyer.

"What the hell did you want in the middle of the night?" he asked.

I kept my eye on Vanilla while I spoke. "A guy named Paul Sanders broke in here last night."

"What happened?"

"I had the drop on him, but he got away. Then Slate's lady friend showed up. She's here now."

"Well, well. Isn't that cozy for you? Don't let her leave, I'll be right over."

I hung up the phone, and said, "That was the sheriff, Vanilla. He wants to talk to you."

She put the coffeepot down and rubbed her palms along the sides of her pants. "About last night," she said. "I . . . I wasn't quite myself. I don't know what it was, maybe everything coming at—"

"No problem. Anything you didn't want to happen, didn't happen. I'll get the dishes and clean up. The sheriff will be here pretty quick."

"Why does he want to talk to me?"

"You knew Slate. It's not only the locals. The FBI and the Secret Service are probably going to want to know everything you've done for the last few days."

41

Her eyebrows lifted slightly. "Everything? Even last night?"

"You came in the front door. Sanders, that's the name of the guy who crashed out the back windows, left. We had a drink, you went to bed. That's how I'll tell it."

The eyebrows slipped back into place. "Why is it I have a tough time believing men who say they're not going to brag about their sexual prowess?"

"I'm not sure I've got all that much to brag about."

She studied me for a minute, trying to figure out just what I meant by the remark. A smile slowly spread across her face. She stood up, started to leave the room, then stopped, leaning against the door frame. "I guess I can stay here for a day or so, can't I? I could help you look for Jack's manuscript."

"It's fine with me."

I had just enough time for a quick shower before Shroyer showed up. He was dressed in another oversized suit, beige today. He must have gone on a diet recently. His shirt collar could have covered another inch of neck. I showed him where Sanders had gotten into the house.

"Here's a statement he typed and signed before he broke away."

Shroyer read the statement, his eyes bouncing from the document to me, getting harder and harder with each bounce.

"'I Paul Sanders,'" Shroyer read, "'did forcibly break into the residence belonging to Jack Slate. I was advised by one Joseph Wilson that it was his home, and that he had some valuable papers he wanted retrieved. Said papers were his property, however, his wife would not let him have access to the documents. Mr. Nick Polo interrupted me during my search. I did not find said documents, nor did I take anything from the residence. Mr.

42

Polo advised me that the house actually belonged to Mr. Slate. I do not have a current address for Joseph Wilson. I will provide Mr. Polo with said address as soon as I locate Wilson.'

"'I declare under the threat of perjury that the above is true and correct. Signed, Paul Sanders.'

"What the hell kind of shit is this, Polo?"

"I just wanted something to hand my client, Lieutenant."

"Bullshit," he said. "You wanted to play games with this asshole. Why didn't you call us right away?"

"I was about to. Then the girl came driving up front. I thought it might be Sanders's backup. I went out to check. When I was talking to the girl, Sanders jumped out the back windows."

"You just left him there while you went to check, huh?"

I picked Sanders's automatic out of a kitchen drawer. "He put up a fight. He was unconscious. I guess I didn't hit him as hard as I thought I did. Here's his gun."

Shroyer picked the gun up and automatically checked to see if it was loaded.

"I took out the bullets," I said.

"Good thinking," he said, with no attempt to hide his bad humor.

"Do you know this Sanders?" I said.

He slumped down into one of the kitchen chairs. "You play games, then expect me to tell you what I know?"

"I'm cooperating, Lieutenant. I just had him type the statement to keep my client happy. It's not easy when you get away from civil service. I called your office. You weren't in. I told them it was important."

"There was nothing on the note I was given. Just

43

your name and the time." He grunted, then leaned back in his chair. "Give me one good reason why I should trust you."

"You know you're not going to get much cooperation from Andrew Burke and the rest of the federal boys. Besides, I've got an expense account. We could have dinner. Your clothes look like they need filling."

"Yeah." He plucked at his waistband. "Cancer. Hard way to diet. Prostate. A real pain in the ass, but they say they got it all." His lips extended in a thoughtful pout. "Sanders is a big, dumb bastard. Local boy. Was a pretty good high school football player. Didn't have the grades to go to college. He boxed for a while, won the first few fights, then started getting the hell kicked out of him. Then he went into the marines. When he got out he got a job serving subpoenas down south. Somehow he got a private investigator's license. Hung out his shingle about six months ago. I don't know how the hell he made a living at it. Kid couldn't find his ass with both hands."

"He claimed this Wilson character paid him three hundred dollars in cash to crash in here, look for 'a book he was writing,' and see who was staying there with his ex-wife."

"And he didn't know where this Wilson guy lived?"

"Said he was staying in some motel in Carmel. Came to Sanders's office with his story."

Shroyer pulled at the loose flesh under his chin. "What do you make of it?" he asked.

"Whoever sent Sanders in here was probably outside somewhere, within binocular distance, casing the place, just waiting to see what happened."

"Makes sense. Where's the girl?"

"Upstairs in her room."

"You two spend the night together?"

44

"There are two bedrooms, Lieutenant. I slept in the spare."

Shroyer started to say something, but the sound of a car pulling up in front of the house stopped him. He peeked out the kitchen window.

"Burke and company. Shit."

6

Burke had one man with him, a tall, stoop-shouldered guy with thick salt-and-pepper hair and a mournful look on his face. They huddled with Shroyer for a few minutes, then they all trooped into the kitchen. I sipped at my coffee as Burke leaned over the table and stared down at me with a contemptuous look on his face. He ran a finger inside his shirt collar, the finger came out wet with sweat.

"Where's the woman?" he asked.

"Upstairs."

"I haven't got time to fool around with you this morning, Polo. Tell me everything that happened last night."

"Who's he?" I asked, pointing a finger at his companion.

"Never mind who he is, just talk to me."

I scraped my chair back and poured myself a little more coffee. "If we're going to get officious again, I think

46

I'll wait until Mr. Gilleran gets back before I answer any questions."

The tall guy walked over and extended his hand. "I'm Terry Wallace of the Secret Service, sir. Your cooperation would be appreciated."

Imagine that? A polite fed. I told them the same story I'd told Shroyer. Burke got all hot and bothered over the statement I had Paul Sanders type and sign.

"I won't tolerate any prima-donna shit from you, Polo. What do you know about this Vanilla Hale?"

"Only what she told me, and that wasn't much."

"Go get her. We'll interview her in the office."

I was happy to comply, because that was one of the rooms that John Henning had bugged.

Vanilla looked nervous when I found her in her room. She was wearing red slacks and a stiffly starched white shirt.

"How long will this take?" she asked.

"Not too long. Just tell them the truth. Don't leave anything out."

She arched an eyebrow.

"Anything pertinent. From what I told them, you might as well be a nun on a retreat."

She smiled, showing a lot of teeth. "All this is making me nervous. And hungry."

"Lunch and dinner are on me."

She took my hand and gave it a hard squeeze.

I was exiled back to the kitchen while they interrogated Vanilla. I guess Shroyer got kicked out too, because in about fifteen minutes he joined me.

"There's something I forgot to tell you, Lieutenant," I said.

"I'll bet there's a lot you've forgot to tell me, Polo."

47

"I saw Slate pack a camera with a telephoto lens onto the plane. Did you check the film?"

"Yeah, we checked. It was all raw. Not a picture taken."

"Did you happen to check the local film developers to see if he had put in any film to be developed?"

"What's this got to do with the something you forgot to tell me?" he said, fiddling with the waistband of his trousers.

"I found Vanilla Hale poking around in Slate's office this morning. She told me that he used to like to play games with trivia names when he was researching a book. He'd use names like Miles Archer and Felix Leiter."

He looked puzzled. I explained who Archer and Leiter were.

"Yeah," he said. "Slate would be one of those jerks that liked to play silly games." He took a notebook out of his pocket and asked me to spell Leiter.

"Thanks for the tip, Polo. We did check under his name, but there was nothing. I'll check these out. Earlier you mentioned an expense account."

"What did you have in mind?"

"Dinner tonight, with you and the girl."

"You're on."

"I'll make the reservations," he said. "Anton and Michael's, in Carmel, at eight."

He started for the door, then turned on his heel. "We're through with Slate's Jaguar. You want to pick it up?"

"Fine. It looks like I'm going to be ignored around here."

I followed him out to his car. He was silent while we drove to the sheriff's garage. His face had that set-in-stone look, so I didn't bother trying to strike up a conversation.

As he pulled the car to a stop, he reached into his pocket, took out a card, and scribbled something on it.

"Give it to Mark, the head mechanic. He'll give you the car."

I thanked him, got out of the car, and when I'd walked a few feet, he beeped his horn and waved me back.

"Were you wondering why that Secret Service agent, Wallace, showed up?"

"Seems natural. They've got to be interested."

"They're more interested than ever. Tom Dykstra's home was in Los Angeles. His wife was found this morning. Dead. Shot three times. Twice in the heart and once in the back of the head."

He put the car in gear and took off, leaving me standing there with a dumb look on my face.

I handed Mark the card Shroyer had given me and drove to the nearest service station to top off the Jag's tank. Driving the Jag was a bit clumsy at first, sitting on the right, shifting with the left hand, and getting the clutch and brake pedals mixed up, but it was a hell of a lot of fun to drive, once I got the hang of it.

I used the service station's pay phone to call Gilleran. He was out of his office, but I left a message with his secretary, passing on the news about Dykstra's wife being murdered.

There are four toll gates leading into Pebble Beach and its famed 17 Mile Drive: Country Club Gate and Lighthouse Gate in Pacific Grove, the Highway 1 Gate, and the Carmel Gate. Each has a little shack manned twenty-four hours a day by a uniformed guard in a Smokey the Bear hat. The fee to get in is five bucks, which is refunded if you eat or shop at the Del Monte Lodge. At five bucks, it's a hell of a bargain. Pebble

Beach, over eight thousand acres of the most expensive real estate in the world. Where jade-color fairways meet the turquoise sea. Views that put the French Riviera to shame: magnificent mansions, a rugged shoreline where you can watch whales blow off steam and seals sunbathe and bark at each other. Five of the most beautiful and toughest golf courses in the world. Whoever it was who first said "rich is better" probably lived in Pebble Beach.

The guard saw the red tournament parking ticket on the Jag's window, smiled, told me to be sure to have a nice day, and waved me through. I pointed the Jag's dignified nose toward the Del Monte Lodge. The lodge's parking lot was overflowing. A clean-cut looking kid saw the sticker, found me a parking spot that was reserved for the golfers. I stopped in at the Tap Room for a hot brandy, finished my drink, helped myself to a handful of pretzels, and set off to find Tregenza, the man the newspaper said was the head gardener for the golf course.

The sun was breaking through the clouds and was warming things up considerably. I walked past the famed eighteenth green, down the fairway, stopping at an area roughly forty square yards, roped off and marked "ground under repair." Four workmen were resodding the grass.

"Would one of you gentlemen be Mr. Tregenza?" I asked.

One of the men, short, compactly built, in his fifties, lifted his head and asked, "Who wants him?"

I held out the police inspector's badge I had never turned in when I left the department, keeping a thumb over the words "San Francisco."

Tregenza leaned on his shovel. "Christ, not another one. I've told my story a dozen times. What now?"

"I know all of this is a pain in the ass, Mr. Tregenza, but I've only got a few questions."

50

He reached into his battered work jacket, pulled out a twisted black rope of a cigar, clamped it between his teeth, and fired it up with a Zippo lighter.

"Get on with them, then," he said through a haze of dirty gray smoke.

"Just where were you when you first saw the plane?"

Tregenza pointed to the east. "By the sixteenth green. He was flying low. I heard the engine, you know, normal like. It's real quiet that time of the morning. Then there was some kind of a popping noise. I looked up, there were flames coming out of the engine." Tregenza joined his hands, fanning the fingers out. "It kind of fluttered like this," he said, wriggling the fingers, "then started down."

"Could you tell where he had been before? Where he was coming from?"

Tregenza shrugged his shoulders. "No. I didn't pay any attention to him till just before he crashed."

"Then what?"

"Then he started coming down fast. Looked like he was trying for a landing." He looked over his shoulder at the three men working on the damaged fairway. "I'm lucky he didn't put it down right in the middle of the seventeenth green."

I tried to figure whether he was joking or serious. He didn't look like a joker. "Yes, you certainly were lucky. A lot luckier than they were. Were you the first one to get to the plane?"

"Sure. There was a hell of a smell of gas. I was afraid it was going to blow up. It only took one look to see they were both dead. Blood all over the place. The one guy, not the pilot, the other guy, his head went right into the windshield."

Tregenza's cigar had gone out and he went through

the production of lighting it again. "Anything else you want, Mr. Policeman?"

"What about the plane itself? Notice anything unusual?"

"Unusual?" He scratched his scalp. "It was almost broken in two. Gas and blood all over the place. That unusual enough for you?"

"Did anyone else come on the scene right away?"

"Nah. No one else around. I ran to the clubhouse, called the police. By the time I got back there was a crowd."

"Anyone else get to the plane before the police arrived?"

"Who knows?" he said, obviously bored with the conversation. "I've got to get back to work. We've got a golf tournament starting up soon."

"Right. First things first."

Tregenza either didn't notice or didn't care about the caustic reply. He picked up his shovel and rejoined his three coworkers.

I looked up into the sky. The airport would be in a southeasterly direction. Where the hell had Slate been heading? There was nothing farther west except the Pacific Ocean. If Slate and Dykstra were planning on taking pictures of something, it had to be between the golf course and the airport. What was so important to get them out that early in the morning? I was brought out of my thoughts by someone tugging at my sleeves.

A thin young woman wearing a "Save the Whales" sweatshirt pointed out to the ocean. "Look at that, isn't that something?" she said.

I scanned the water, wondering what she was talking about.

"Right there! By the rocks. See him?"

A sea otter was contentedly floating on his back, the glistening inner shell of an abalone resting on the light fur of his stomach.

"Beautiful, isn't it?" asked the woman.

"Not to the abalone," I said, suddenly thinking of lunch and Vanilla Hale.

7

"You call this lunch?" asked Vanilla Hale, wrinkling her nose in distaste at the bag of McDonald's hamburgers.

"I thought we'd have a big dinner, and I didn't want to spoil your appetite."

She opened the bag, her long fingers picking up a hamburger, holding it as if it were a mouse that might bite her. "I think I'll pass on lunch." She dropped the burger onto the kitchen table. "I hope you have something more elaborate planned for dinner."

"Nothing but the best," I said. "There will be three of us though. The sheriff wanted to join us."

I thought she'd balk at seeing the law again, but she just nodded. "As long as there's real food."

I grabbed a bottle of beer from the refrigerator and dug into a Big Mac.

"How did you get along with the feds?"

"How does anyone get along with them? They told me about that Secret Service agent's wife being murdered." She sat down abruptly, palms flat on her thighs, eyes staring blankly at the floor. "They just asked questions and I answered them."

"I bet."

"I told them that I had flown up here with Jack a few days ago, got bored and went back to Palm Springs. I had never heard of that man Dykstra. I don't know what Jack did after I left for Palm Springs."

"Didn't he call you?"

"Yes. Once. He said everything was fine. He wanted me to come back, to be around when he played in the golf tournament. Sort of a cheerleader. Jack always likes people rooting for him."

"How good a pilot was Slate?"

"The scary kind," she said. "Jack flew pretty much like he did everything else. He liked taking chances. While it was new and he was learning, he was careful, cautious. But once he figured he was in control, knew what he was doing, he got bored and had to liven things up."

"Was he like that with women too?"

She responded with a forced grin. "All men are like that when it comes to women."

"Did he ever do much drinking when he was flying?" I asked, remembering the coffee cup smelling of booze that I'd found in Slate's car.

"He usually had a few drinks before everything."

"Drugs?"

"A little grass. Some coke. He fooled around with chemicals years ago, before I met him. Claimed it was research for a book he was writing. Of course, he said everything he was doing had something to do with a book he was writing."

I stood up, brushing crumbs from my pant legs. "Come on, let's go for a ride."

"Where to?"

"The airport. You can stay here if you want, but I wouldn't be surprised if the feds came back for another chat."

"You certainly do know how to persuade a girl," she said, rising up, arching her shoulders and stretching her arms behind her. I probably could have heard some bones cracking, but I wasn't concentrating on her bones.

"Let me get a jacket," she said, and went upstairs.

"Mind if I drive?" Vanilla asked when we got to the Jag. We both seemed to prefer it to our rental cars.

I tossed her the keys. "Be my guest."

"The sun's out," she said, unsnapping the convertible top. "Let's enjoy this ride."

She manipulated the steering wheel and gearshift with easy, professional movements, and I felt my spine press into the back of the bucket seat as she skidded around the corner and accelerated down the road.

Sunny or not, I pulled up my collar to ward off the chill wind. "You and Slate must have been quite a pair. He flies when he's drunk and you drive like you're at Le Mans."

She took a turn too fast and the tires squealed in protest as she braked and shifted into second gear.

"Listen, if you're mad about something, take it out on me, not the car," I said.

She ignored me and the speedometer was soon

hovering past the seventy-five mark, then, as we approached a shopping area, she slowed down.

"You're right. This is too nice a car to be mad at."

She handled the Jag with cool competence for the rest of the trip, not speaking a word. When she pulled into the Carmel Valley Airfield, she parked, then got out, slamming the door behind her with a lot more force than was necessary.

The airport hadn't changed much since my last visit.

"Looks like a fucking cow pasture, doesn't it?" Vanilla said.

I had to grin. It was a pretty accurate description.

"When was it that you and Slate first flew up here?"

"A week ago today. It was in the afternoon, around two o'clock."

She dug in her purse for a cigarette.

"Where did Slate park the plane?"

"Over there, by the blue-and-white one."

When I saw Slate climb into the plane it had been parked about four stalls away from where Vanilla was pointing. Which meant that he had taken the plane on another cruise between the time he first arrived and the day he died.

The airport was deserted again.

Vanilla was leaning against the car, her arms crossed, her face crumpled in a rueful smile.

I said, "After you landed here, how did you get to the house?"

"Jack called for a cab."

A battered red Ford pickup drove by us and parked next to one of the planes. The driver, a tall, muscular young man in Levi's and a plaid shirt, gave us a curious glance, then took a toolbox from the truck's bed and opened the plane's engine cowling.

"I found a coffee cup that smelled of whiskey in the back of the Jag the morning he flew off with Dykstra," I said.

She pulled a face as if she'd suddenly bitten into a sour lemon. "Jack could handle the booze. I'd be afraid to fly with him when he wasn't drinking. He'd get the shakes if he stayed on the wagon for more than a couple of days."

"What about photography? Was he interested in cameras?"

"Cameras? He had dozens of them. It was another of his hobbies. He was always taking pictures." She dropped her cigarette in the dirt, grinding it under her heel. "Did the police find any pictures at the house?"

"Not that I know of. Why? Should they have?"

She shrugged her shoulders and stared at the ground.

"So you land here, call a cab, then what?"

"Then we go to his house. It was very musty smelling. Jack hadn't been there for a while, and I'd never been there before. Jack went with the cabby to get some food and a battery."

"Battery?"

Her hand affectionately patted the Jaguar's hood. "For the car. He had it stored in the garage with the battery and rotor missing. Said he was going to restore it one of these days."

"What did Slate bring with him? I mean other than the usual clothes?"

She nibbled at the inside of her cheek. "Nothing unusual, just his cameras, golf clubs, some Maui wowie, his gun."

"Gun?"

58

"Oh, sure. Macho Jack wouldn't go around without his six-shooter." She glanced at her wristwatch. "Let's get out of here. It gives me the creeps."

"In a minute," I said, walking over to the man working on his plane. "Hi. When does the airport manager usually show up?"

He inclined his head slightly. "Very seldom. You another cop?"

"No, why? Have they been questioning you?"

"Yeah, yesterday."

"I'm an insurance investigator, Nick Polo's the name."

"Mike Kelly," he said, putting down a wrench and rubbing his hand on his jeans before shaking.

His plane was a tiny Piper Cub. It looked like a strong gust of wind could tear it apart.

"Nice plane," I said. "You ever charter it out?"

"You a pilot?" he asked.

"No, but I'd like to take a little ride. Right now. Over toward Pebble Beach."

"You mean where Slate crashed?"

"Right. It's worth a hundred dollars."

Kelly smiled. "Mister, you just rented yourself an airplane. It'll take me about five minutes to get ready."

I went back to the car. "I'm going to take a little airplane ride."

Vanilla glanced at her watch again.

"Take the car," I said. "I'll meet you back at the house. Don't forget about dinner. Anton and Michael's at eight o'clock."

"After skipping lunch, how could I forget about dinner?" she said, climbing into the Jag.

I tried to get comfortable in the Piper Cub's cramped

seat. The truth was that I could never get comfortable in the first-class section of a 747. I'm one of those "if God wanted us to fly, he would have given us wings" types. A scholar once said that it wasn't the flying that scared him, it was taking off and landing. I agreed a hundred percent, but with one addition. Flying over water. I figured that if something happened there was always a chance the plane could limp into a close airport, or land on a freeway, or something, but water. All it was was wet and deep and full of sharks. I wondered what Slate and Dykstra were thinking about during those last few seconds.

Kelly gave a running narrative as he taxied the plane for a takeoff. "From what I understand, Slate took off around sunrise. It was clear, good visibility."

I closed my eyes.

"Slate's plane was a little fancier than this," continued Kelly, as the Piper's propellers bit into the wind. "Not much of an airport, is it? They built it during World War II and stocked it with a few P-38 fighters that patrolled the coast looking for the Japanese invasion. Must have been good duty."

I could feel the plane lift off the ground. I opened my eyes. "Could you circle around here for a minute?"

I spotted the light-blue Jaguar speeding down the road toward Carmel. "What about radio contact?" I asked Kelly over the drone of the engine.

"He wouldn't have needed any as long as he didn't bother the approach paths at Monterey Peninsula Airport. He could fly under the approach level with no problems. That's what I'd do. No sense chattering if you don't have to."

"How high are we flying?"

"We're up two thousand feet. I'll level her off at twenty-five hundred."

The ground below was a beautiful mixture of greens and browns.

"The way I figure it," said Kelly, "the bomb was set up to the altimeter."

"What makes you so sure there was a bomb?"

"It was on the noon news. No doubt about it, they said. Besides, you could tell by the way the cops were asking questions. Had to be a bomb. Whoever did it did it right. Didn't want it to go off on a timer. Too risky. Guy might get engine trouble, not get off, all kinds of things could happen. But with the altimeter, he'd set it on a double hook, at, oh, say one thousand feet. That way it wouldn't go off on takeoff, plane could blow, but he might land soft, even have time to get back to the airfield. No, set it up so that when he was coming in somewhere, or just dropping low to look at the girls on the beach, then wham!" Kelly brought his hands together in a resounding clap. "Use a little trisynol or some good plastic explosive."

"You seem to know a lot about bombs."

"Got the army to thank for that. Good thing you picked today for the flight. They might not let us over here tomorrow."

"Why not?"

"The Goodyear blimp is coming over later today, getting ready for the golf tournament. Those shots they get from up here look dandy on television, don't they?"

We were over Pebble Beach now. I could see the golf course in its entirety, stretching along the water and into the beautiful forest.

"Say that Slate was interested in taking some pictures from his plane. How low could he fly?"

Kelly pointed the nose of the plane down. "Oh, let's

61

say we could get away with five hundred feet. Especially at that time of the morning."

The golf course disappeared from sight, replaced by beautiful, secluded homes. The ocean, a golf course, and houses. There was really nothing else. So Slate and Dykstra wanted to take an early-morning look at a house. But which one? And why?

I told Kelly I'd seen enough and we headed back to Carmel Valley Airfield. For another twenty bucks, Kelly agreed to drive me back to Carmel.

8

Both Vanilla and the Jag were missing when I got back to the house. She'd left a note on the kitchen table.

"See you at dinner at eight." Signed with a big, sloppy *V* that took up the whole bottom of the page.

I went to Slate's office and retrieved the recorder John Henning had set up. Thanks to the complete chaos of the room, Henning didn't have much trouble in hiding the recorder. The microphone itself was hooked into the telephone and was voice-actuated, which meant that it would pick up anything going on in the room and both sides of telephone conversations.

I rewound the tape and listened to Vanilla's interrogation by Burke and Terry Wallace, the Secret Service agent. They played good cop, bad cop with her, or maybe that was their natural personalities. Anyway, Burke came on stronger than industrial-strength cleanser, while Wallace remained cool and smooth.

They went over Vanilla's story thoroughly, cross-checking her movements, in Monterey, Palm Springs, and Los Angeles, where she and Slate had spent a couple of weeks at the Beverly Hills Hotel.

I took notes, though there really didn't seem to be much there that would be of any help in locating Slate's manuscript, and Vanilla swore up and down that she had never heard of Dykstra and had never heard Slate talk about any Secret Service agents. "He never told me anything about his work," she said, over and over.

I continued scribbling after their interview was over, and reached for the phone when I heard it ringing, only the phone line was dead. The ringing was coming from the tape. Six rings. A delay while the recorder shut itself off, then another half a dozen rings. This sequence repeated itself five times: six rings, with the delay in between when the voice-noise–activated recorder turned itself off.

Finally there was the sound of someone running across the floor, then a voice, Vanilla's, sounding out of breath.

"Yes, hello," she said.

There was a series of beeps, seven of them, like someone punching in a telephone number. Then Vanilla said, "I'll be there in half an hour." There was a banging as she hung up the receiver. Then she said, "Shit." Followed by the sounds of retreating footsteps.

I leaned back in Slate's leather chair and listened for more, but that's all there was. And what the hell was it that was there? I ran the tape back and played the beeps over and over. I picked up the phone and started punching out numbers, trying to find the ones that would correspond to the beeps on the tape, but it was useless. I couldn't tell which were which. And even if I did, where would that leave me? I'd lost my Captain Midnight secret decoder years ago.

Vanilla, my dear, just what the hell are you up to?

The phone rang and startled me. It actually was the phone this time.

"That you, Polo?"

It was Jim Gilleran's voice.

"Yes. I tried calling you this morning," I said.

"I've been busy as hell. What's going on?"

I told Gilleran about what had happened since he left. "It looks like there was a bomb on the plane."

"Jesus, a bomb. And Dykstra's wife being murdered. Maybe whoever did this was after Dykstra all the time, and Slate just got in the way. Stay on top of it, Nick. Slate's editor said that Slate was always writing down notes, and that if he had something going with Dykstra, he would have put it down on paper somewhere. Find the notes, and the manuscript, buddy, and there's a hell of a bonus in it for you."

"How much hell of a are we talking?"

Gilleran's voice always changed when the subject of money came up. It got deeper, as if he'd have to go deep down into a vault to get it.

"Well, I'm not talking about myself, Nick, but the publisher let it be known that they would be willing to pay up to twenty-five thousand dollars for something really hot."

Which meant that they were talking a lot more, because Gilleran would have his hand in there first.

"Okay, Jim, I'll keep at it. Do me a favor. Talk to those publishing people. See if they have any information on Slate's latest girlfriend." I spelled her name out for him, and he made what in the sexual discrimination law-

65

suits is called a typical male sexist remark. One I imagine the comely Miss Hale had heard several hundred times.

"Vanilla, huh? Knowing Slate I bet she's good enough to eat."

"Careful, remember this line is bugged. If she got hold of the tape, she could sue you for that."

"That's the trouble with the law. It's got no sense of humor. Keep in touch."

I had barely hung up when the phone chirped again. This time it was Lieutenant Shroyer.

"Is dinner still on?" he asked.

"Yes, why, is there a problem?"

"Maybe. Come on over to Paul Sanders's house, 1431 Eighth Street in Monterey, and I'll spoil your appetite."

My rental car had come equipped with maps, so I had no trouble finding 8th Street. There were two squad cars and the same gray Chrysler Shroyer had been driving that morning parked in front of a small, whitewashed bungalow that looked like it had been built in the forties. A pair of battered shutters hung drunkenly from around a bay window.

A group of curious neighbors were gathered a few feet away from the front entrance. They gave me suspicious glances as I parked and got out of my car.

There must have been a park nearby. I could hear the sound of a tennis ball being batted back and forth.

A young patrolman stopped me as I mounted the first of three cement steps leading to the house. He had a pressed uniform, a shiny badge, and shinier shoes. He was still new enough to be impressed with himself and the job.

"My name's Polo. Lieutenant Shroyer sent for me."

66

"Wait here, please," he asked politely.

The front door was wide open. The hardwood floor was rubbed down to bare wood in spots. A neglected wandering Jew sat dying of thirst in a big clay pot just inside the door.

"Okay, you can go in," said the uniform when he returned.

I followed the small hallway, passed a kitchen with a white enamel stove and refrigerator, down to the point of interest. There were at least four people crowded into the garage. Five if you counted the guy on the floor.

Shroyer waved a hand. "Come on in." He pointed to the floor. "Recognize him?"

I took a deep breath. Even the poor bastard's mother would have a tough time recognizing him. Only his size and hair resembled the man I had seen just last night. I pulled my eyes away and looked at Shroyer. "You didn't need me to make an ID." I turned on my heel and walked out to the kitchen. One of the windows was wide open. I stuck my head out and sucked in deep drafts of air.

"Pretty ugly, huh?" Shroyer said when I pulled my head back in.

"Yeah, you could certainly say that. What are we doing here, Shroyer, playing games? You interested to see if I can handle the sight of someone that's had his head turned into Jell-O? Well, if it makes you feel better, the answer is no. I've seen more than my share of dead bodies, some a lot worse than that poor bastard, but I never got to where it didn't bother me. Satisfied?"

"Calm down, will you? I wasn't playing games. I don't like looking at the remains any more than you do. But it's my job, Polo, and I'm good at my job. That piece of mangled meat in there is Paul Sanders, and as of right

67

now you're the last person I know of that saw him alive and you admitted roughing him up."

"I bopped him a couple of times, I told you that, but he certainly wasn't in that kind of shape when he left Slate's place."

Shroyer opened the refrigerator door, took a quick peek, then slammed it shut.

"If you had called us right away, kept him at Slate's place, he wouldn't be dead right now."

My hands were shaking, so I kept them in my pockets. It was times like this that I regretted giving up smoking. You get nervous, the first place you show it is your hands.

"Don't lay any guilt trips on me, Shroyer. Sanders was a big boy. He got mixed up with someone bigger."

He took a small tablet from his pocket, flipped a few sheets over, then said, "The coroner says it looks like he took some hits from something heavy, either a sap or a piece of pipe. Finished him off with a coat hanger around the neck."

"Neighbors?"

"Heard nothing, as usual. Probably got to him when he came into the garage. Probably right after he got away from you." Shroyer looked at me expectantly. "Got anything to tell me?"

"I gave you everything I had this morning, Lieutenant."

"So you'll be leaving soon?"

"A couple of days. They want me to tie up some loose ends."

"Such as?"

"Estate problems. I heard about the bomb."

Shroyer coughed, phlegm rattling in his throat. "Yeah, this is really something, isn't it? Bombs, plane

68

crashes, famous authors, beautiful women, seedy private eyes, one of whom gets himself killed. It would make a good movie, wouldn't it?"

"Terrific," I agreed. "You don't need me around here any more, do you, Lieutenant?"

"I don't really think I need you at all, Polo," he said, walking back toward the bedroom. He stopped at the door and gave me a crooked grin. "Except for dinner tonight. Don't forget the girl."

9

"Don't forget the girl." Good advice. Apparently Andrew Burke, intrepid FBI man, wasn't sharing Vanilla with Shroyer, and he figured that he could get to her through me. Me and my expense account.

I went back to Slate's place. There was still no sign of her.

I started rummaging through Slate's desk again, then riffled though the pages of every one of his books, looking for any kind of handwritten note relating to Dykstra. Vanilla had said that he would write on matchbooks, cocktail napkins, anything. I couldn't find a word. Maybe the feds had beat me to it, maybe it simply wasn't there.

Gilleran was sending a man down to Palm Springs to check Slate's house there. Maybe he'd have more luck. The only thing I was turning up was dustballs.

Something was missing obviously, but what? If Slate was such a demon for writing things down, he'd have to

70

have put down something about his meeting with Dykstra.

I gave up and walked into town and picked up the local newspaper, had a cup of coffee in a Scandinavian tea shop, and learned a lot more about former Secret Service agent Thomas Dykstra from the paper than I had from either Burke or Shroyer.

Dykstra had been in the service for almost thirty years and had been assigned to numerous presidents: Kennedy, Johnson, Nixon, Ford, and Carter. He had been with Ford for the last four years, which must have been something of a boring existence.

There was nothing new on the murder of Dykstra's wife. The newspaper story said that Dykstra's house had been ransacked and that burglary was a possibility. At least that was the story the police were putting out. Buy that and we'll talk about a good deal on the Golden Gate bridge.

The one thing of interest in the article was that Dykstra had been with former President Ford in Palm Springs for the Bob Hope Golf Classic a few weeks before. Vanilla said that she and Slate were there also. So that would have been the perfect time for Dykstra and Slate to meet. I was sure that Burke and the Secret Service agent, Terry Wallace, were digging into that angle.

Dykstra sees Slate, does he bump into him? Or seek him out? Or was it the other way around? Slate sees Dykstra. It wasn't exactly hard to spot a Secret Service man when he's protecting an ex-president, especially around a golf course. You can only hide so much of a shoulder holster and walkie-talkie under a cardigan. Somehow they meet. Why? Dykstra was a career man. Slate wouldn't be the type of guy that most people in the Secret Service would warm up to. His book making public

71

the identity of CIA agents in foreign embassies had rankled just about every type of G-man there is. Three agents had been killed, two in Greece and one in Chile, after their names popped up in Slate's book. So what would bring these two opposites together? Palm Springs may have been accidental, but what about again in Pebble Beach?

I dug through the sports page. There was a list of the celebrities who were expected to play at Pebble Beach. Gerald Ford wasn't listed; Dykstra must have been up here on his own, meeting with Slate in the early-morning hours, flying low over a golf course. Golf seemed to be the common denominator.

I walked back to Slate's house, passing the Carmel post office. It's another one of the town's charms that no one gets mail delivered to the house. One of the reasons is that there are no addresses per se. You don't live at 123 Elm Street, because there are no house numbers. You live at the brown shingle place near the corner of Dolores, and to get your mail you have to go to the post office and pick it up every day. Very continental, very "old worldish." That's why the post office is such a popular gathering place. Sooner or later, everyone in town stops by to pick up the mail. I wondered if Slate had anything in his postal box. Burke and Wallace would have that covered.

There was still no sign of Vanilla Hale when I got back to Slate's place. I waited until almost eight, then drove down to town.

Anton and Michael's was busy. The air was perfumed with scents of garlic, spices, and expensive wines. The maître d' led me to our table. Lieutenant Shroyer was already seated, as was Vanilla. She was wearing a black, low-cut silk dress, held up by spaghetti straps. She had on long matching black gloves that gave her an erotic

72

look that reminded me of Rita Hayworth in *Gilda*. If Vanilla was in mourning, she was certainly doing it in style.

"You two seem to be getting along," I said, sliding into the chair the maître d' pulled out for me.

"Glad you could make it," Shroyer said in a voice that didn't even try to sound sincere.

Vanilla gave me a wide smile. "The lieutenant and I were just about to order a drink." She turned the smile to Shroyer. "I don't think I can call you Lieutenant all night. What is your first name?"

"Elmer."

She raised her eyebrows amiably. "What are you drinking, Lieutenant?"

Shroyer must have been wearing a postoperation suit. It actually fit him. "Club soda," he said.

"Beefeater martini," she told the hovering waiter.

"Make that two martinis," I added.

"How did you get along with the FBI, Miss Hale?" Shroyer asked.

"They were polite. Thorough, but polite."

"Did Polo tell you about Paul Sanders?"

She tilted her head. "Sanders?"

"The man who broke into Slate's house just before you arrived last night. We found him today. Murdered, in his garage."

"Fuck," said Vanilla, startling the waiter as he was setting our drinks on the table.

No one spoke as Vanilla peeled off her gloves. Every male eye in the restaurant was watching the black silk slide down those long arms. She picked up her drink, took a long swallow, then mumbled something about going to the powder room.

"The news about Sanders seemed to shake her up," Shroyer said, plucking the olive from my martini.

73

"Death does that to some people."

"Did she say she knew Sanders?"

"Not to me. She never even got a look at him last night."

When Vanilla came back to the table, she drained what was left in her glass, then said to Shroyer, "I imagine this wasn't meant to be purely a social event, Lieutenant. Just what did you want to ask me?"

"Miss Hale, why don't you tell me everything you can about what happened from the time you and Jack Slate first flew into town?"

Vanilla and I went through another round of drinks and a goodly portion of a bottle of Taittinger Comtes de Champagne before she was through with her story. Shroyer had taken me at my word on the expense account. He insisted on doing the ordering: Blue Point oysters, rack of lamb, Limestone lettuce salad, and Cherries Jubilee for dessert. I felt more than slightly bloated when the coffee came.

"What have you found out about Jack?" Vanilla asked, after the table had been cleared.

"Not much. Not much at all, Miss Hale."

I signaled to the waiter, put my Visa card near my coffee cup, and said, "I'll be right back."

There was a pay phone by the men's room. I called John Henning in San Francisco.

"John, I need a favor." I gave him the number for Anton and Michael's. "As soon as I hang up, call, ask for a Miss Vanilla Hale. If there's any confusion, tell whoever answers the phone that she's with Lieutenant Shroyer. When she gets on the phone, don't say a thing. Just push seven buttons on your phone. Like this." I pushed the buttons on my phone.

"It doesn't make any sense," Henning said.

74

"Not to me. Maybe it will to her. Don't say anything. Just push any seven buttons, then hang up. I'll call you later."

When I got back to the table Shroyer had ordered coffee for himself and Vanilla.

The suave maître d' came to the table, bent discreetly over Vanilla's shoulder, and, careful not to let his eyes wander down her decolletage, said, "A phone call for you, madam."

She seemed puzzled. We watched her walk away.

"Well, Shroyer. What do you think?"

"I think she knows a hell of a lot more than she's saying. But I think the same thing about you, Polo." He patted his stomach. "Thanks for dinner."

"My expense account's pleasure."

"We ran those two names you gave us through the local photo developers, Felix Leiter and the other guy." He snapped his fingers several times while waiting for the name to pop into his memory. "Archer, Miles Archer. No luck, but guess what? Someone else was calling and asking if either of those two gentlemen had left some pictures in to be developed."

"Man or a woman do the calling?" I asked.

"Man. Pesty bugger. One guy says he's sure the same man called and had him check under the name Charles Allnut."

"Doesn't mean anything to me," I said. "Maybe it will to Vanilla."

"Why do you think she's sticking around?" he asked.

"I thought you or Burke has asked, or insisted, that she do so."

He leaned back, emitted a slight burp, and smiled. "You mean, 'don't leave town'? I don't have enough juice

75

to tell her that. Maybe Burke does, but he doesn't confide in me completely."

"Maybe she just wants to be helpful."

He snorted. "To who? Burke? Me? I think she's working for someone. Maybe she's after the manuscript you're so hot for. I did a little checking on Hale. She is, or was, a legitimate model. Did a lot of covers, *Cosmopolitan*, *Vogue*, that kind of stuff. Even did a *Sports Illustrated* swimsuit issue about ten years ago. Yeah, she's working for someone. It's not just your charm that's keeping her here."

I didn't get a chance to respond. Vanilla returned, looking nervous.

She stood by her chair. "I'm sure you gentlemen have things to talk about." She held out a hand to Shroyer. "Nice talking to you, Lieutenant." I didn't get a hand, just a quick look and an "I'll see you later."

I scribbled a good-size tip on the Visa bill, then stood up. "Thanks, Lieutenant. I'll keep in touch."

"In kind of a hurry, aren't you, Polo? Afraid she'll take off?"

That was exactly what I was afraid of, but I just mumbled something about promising to call Gilleran.

"Keep in touch, Polo," Shroyer said as he picked up his coffee cup.

Parking is always a problem in Carmel. My rental car was a block away. I caught a glimpse of Vanilla as she climbed into the Jaguar. I caught up with her on Ocean Avenue. She was traveling fast, up to Highway 1, heading north. She pulled off on Munras Avenue and drove into Monterey, toward Fisherman's Wharf and the Cannery, pulling into a parking lot by one of the town's better restaurants, The Sardine Factory. She sat and waited. And waited, finally getting out of the car and going to a pay phone. I could see her making arm waving gestures as she spoke. She slammed down the receiver and walked back to the Jaguar, peeling rubber as she pulled out of the lot.

She drove right back to Carmel and Jack Slate's house. I gave her five minutes before I went in. She was upstairs. Her bedroom door was closed. I knocked lightly. There was no response.

10

I found Vanilla sipping coffee in the kitchen the next morning. She was dressed in an off-white cotton flight suit, with zippers at the ankles and wrists, and embroidered patches, one of the American flag, others of what I assumed were combat units of various armies and navies sprinkled around the sleeves and chest. A pair of dark aviation glasses covered her eyes. She looked like something out of a commercial for a Rambo flick.

"Good morning," she said, taking a look at the black oversized watch on her wrist. "I have to go see someone."

"Anyone I know?" I asked, helping myself to a cup of coffee.

"No. It's business. I have to get back to work soon."

"Work?"

"Yes, modeling. And believe me, it's hard work. Will you be here later?"

"Yes, I'm not going anywhere. You know, when I

first saw you, you looked familiar. It must have been that *Sports Illustrated* issue."

She gave me a small smile. "That's the one everyone seems to remember." She put her cup in the sink, took off her glasses, and looked me square in the eye.

"Nick, do you know anything about that phone call I got at the restaurant last night?"

"No. Who was it?"

She kept looking at me, then shrugged, put her sunglasses back on, and smiled. "No one. Just a deep breather. He didn't say a word."

"You feel like some company on your drive? I've got nothing to do this morning."

"No, thanks. I've got to do this alone. See you later."

I watched as she drove off in the Jaguar, then went out to my rental and tried following her again. She made several lefts and rights through Carmel and I lost her. I got on Highway 1 and went back to Monterey, to The Sardine Factory, but there was no sign of the blue Jag.

I drove back to Slate's house and called John Henning, and asked him about his phone call last night.

"I did just what you said, Nick. Punched out those seven numbers."

"And what did she say?"

"Nothing. Not a word."

"Okay, John. Thanks."

I called Jim Gilleran's office. He was out, and his secretary said that they had not found any trace of the missing manuscript at Slate's Palm Springs home.

That left me alone, and bored. I went through the motions of searching the house again.

Around eleven a station wagon pulled up in front of

the house. The stenciling on the car's door said "Pebble Beach Golf Course."

A good-looking kid in his twenties, with hair that was closer to platinum than blond, pulled a red leather golf bag out of the back of the wagon and walked up to the front door.

"This Mr. Slate's house?" he asked.

"Yes, it is."

"These are his clubs."

"Thanks, we were looking for those," I said, taking the bag and closing the door before he started asking questions, like "Who the hell are you?"

I carried the golf bag into the kitchen. It was twice as big as the bag in the garage. I pulled out one of the irons and swung it back and forth slowly. Pings. Top-quality clubs. The grooves were clean, no dirt or grass in those grooves, which is the way it should be. A caddy was mandatory for a tournament like the Hope or the Crosby. The caddy would clean the club after every swing, or go over the whole bag thoroughly after the round was over. I should have known Slate wouldn't have used that old set of clubs I'd found in the garage to play in a tournament.

I dropped the club to the floor and hefted the bag up on the kitchen table. It had several zippered compartments for balls, tees, and scorecards. A larger compartment held a set of white golf shoes, which, like the clubs, were cleaned and polished. I pulled out the shoes, then a windbreaker. There, lying next to a pair of rain pants, was a thick roll of white-and-yellow paper, secured by rubber bands.

I pulled the paper out and ripped off the rubber bands. There must have been over two hundred pages, the majority typed, single-spaced, with words, even whole sentences, *x*'d out. The yellow pages were handwritten in both pencil and ink. I hurried back to the front door, made sure it was locked, went to the closet where I'd put Slate's shotgun, carried it back to the kitchen, made sure it was loaded, then put it gingerly down on the table and began to read.

It took me a couple of hours. According to Slate, the shah had left town with untold billions of dollars, and, when he died, the money disappeared. Slate followed the paper trail from Iran to Switzerland, Mexico, the Bahamas, South America, listing the names of banks, bankers, even the numbers to certain accounts. The notation, "D.C. Money Man," showed up several times. Was D.C. somebody's initials, or did it mean Washington, D.C.? But no mention of Dykstra.

I went back to the golf bag and dug out a pile of scorecards. One card for Spyglass, one of the courses played in the Crosby, for a round of golf played just the day before Slate's crash, had the word "pics" and the letters L.R., printed alongside his score, which by the way was a 94. On the back of the card for a round of golf played three weeks before on the El Dorado Club course in Palm Springs, was the name Dykstra. Next to it was another name. "Zadar!" Just like that. Zadar, followed by an explanation point.

Bingo. Zadar's name had been fairly prominent in the manuscript. I went back to the typed pages, and there he was: Sedez Zadar, former chief of interrogation for SAVAK, Sezemane Etelaat va Aminate Kechvar, the security and intelligence organization of the Iranian state. The shah's CIA.

According to Slate, Zadar had been the man the shah had put in charge when he knew he was going to have to leave Iran. Zadar was the "bag man," assigned to find a suitable living site for the shah until he returned to his country. But the shah didn't live very long after being given the boot. So Zadar must have been left holding the bag. And a heavy bag it must have been.

I celebrated by taking a bottle of Mumm's from the refrigerator. I toasted myself with a full glass before calling Gilleran with the good news.

"His golf bag," Gilleran said. "Why the hell didn't you think of that before?"

"You certainly know how to help a man celebrate. Just be thankful I did think of it, and got out to the golf course and found it before the cops did," I said, feeling justified in telling a small white lie to an attorney. No sense telling him the damn thing had been dropped into my lap.

"Yeah, I guess you're right, Nick. Okay, here's what you do. Go to the offices of Gowan and Marucco, they're a law firm on Hartnell in Monterey. Use their FAX machine and send me a copy of the manuscript right away. Don't let anyone else use the machine. Do it yourself. I'll send a messenger from my office down there right now. Give him the original and all the notes, everything. I want the original."

"What about the police? They'll want to see it."

"I'm sure they will. I'll call the FBI guy, what's his name?"

"Burke."

"Yeah, I'll call him once I've got the original. If he wants to see it, he can come up here. Is there anything in the damn manuscript that sheds any light on the plane crash?"

"Nothing that I could see. Not in the manuscript. I'm sure Burke will be interested in the scorecard with Dykstra and Zadar's name on it."

"Who the hell is Zadar?" Gilleran asked.

"He was the head of SAVAK, the shah's CIA."

"Jesus Christ," Gilleran said. "Shoot me a FAX of the scorecard. And put it in with the book for the messenger. Let's keep quiet about that for now. I'd like to see what we can turn up on this Zadar character. You've done good, Nick. I won't forget it."

"I won't let you. What about the woman?"

"Woman?"

"Vanilla Hale. Did you find out anything about her from Slate's publisher?"

"She was a big-time model once, almost up in the Christie Brinkley, Cheryl Tiegs league, then she kind of dropped from sight. I'll call the publisher now. They're going to go bananas when I tell them I found the manuscript. Get down to Gowan and Marucco's. I can't wait to start reading that damn thing."

I went to the law offices of Gowan and Marucco and used their FAX machine to send up copies of the manuscript and the scorecard with Zadar's name on it to Gilleran, so he could FAX them right back to the publisher in New York. I decided to hold back on the card with the words "pics" and L.R. I wanted to find out just what the hell it meant.

I had the copy machine room all to myself, so I made a Xerox copy of the manuscript and the scorecard with Zadar's name on it. The messenger from Gilleran's office came, I handed him the original manuscript and the Zadar scorecard.

I went back to Slate's house. Vanilla hadn't returned. I was going to tell her the news about the manuscript and drop in Zadar's name, to see how she would react to it.

I was all keyed up, with nowhere to go, anxious to

see her. I read through the copy of the manuscript again, taking down notes on Zadar. He had last showed up in the Bahamas, just before the shah died. Where was he now? Palm Springs? Pebble Beach?

If Dykstra had come up here, it was more than likely Pebble Beach. Was he living here? Or was he just here for the tournament?

I called a friend, Jane Tobin, a reporter at the *San Francisco Bulletin*. She had been one of the pioneering women sports writers and now had her own weekly column.

"Jane, I need a list of all of the professionals and amateurs who played in the Hope golf tournament a couple of weeks ago."

"Whatever for, Nick? Where are you, anyway?"

"Carmel. I'm working on the Jack Slate thing."

I could feel the interest bubble up in her voice. "Oh, really? Got anything I can use?"

"Maybe, but I need that list first."

"What's the connection?" she asked.

"None yet. Did you ever cover golf for the paper?"

"No. They move around too much. All I know is that they make tons of money, and most of them are boring as hell. That Greg Norman is a hunk though. And that youngest Crosby kid is cute."

"You're turning into a sexist. You probably go to the tennis matches just to look at those guys in their shorts."

"No, basketball is better. They have better *tushes*. This may take me a day or so, Nick."

"No problem."

We chatted a couple of minutes about odds and ends, and when we were going to have lunch again. I hung up and there I was with time on my hands once more. If Slate had gotten Zadar's name from Dykstra when they were in Palm Springs, he surely would have done some research. He was too nosy to let it just lie. What the hell would he do? Try to find him, peg him down. It would make a much better book if he could nail Zadar. So Slate would play detective.

Shroyer said that whoever had called asking about Miles Archer and Felix Leiter had also asked about someone called Charles Allnut. I'd forgotten to ask Vanilla if that was one of Slate's phony names.

I went to the library and found the *Trivia Encyclopedia* that Vanilla had been paging through the previous morning. It was listed as Charlie Allnut, the role Humphrey Bogart played in *The African Queen*.

Well, there was no faulting Slate's imagination. He was a man after my own heart. I had spent a happily depraved life as a teenager checking into motels under the name George Walker, the name my comic book hero, The Phantom, used when he left the jungle and wandered into civilization.

So Slate loved word games. The scorecard with "pics" had the letters L.R. on it. Using what was left of my little gray cells, I figured Slate may have put a roll of film in to be developed under a name with the initials L.R.

I looked down the list in the trivia book at all the roles Bogart had played in the movies. No L.R. Then I started down the listings under L. There was Lash La Rue. But that was L.L.R. Besides, the name Lash was a little too much even for Slate.

I started back down the *L*s again and went past old names I hadn't seen in years, Lew Archer, Lieutenant Jacoby, Little Beaver, and Lois Lane, before I came to a real L.R. Lone Ranger: secret identity of Texas Ranger

John Reid. Jack Slate. The Lone Ranger. It was worth a chance.

I went to the phone book and hit pay dirt on the fourteenth call. Long's Drugs at the shopping center at the Crossroads had three rolls of film under Mr. John Reid's name.

I stopped at a camera store in Carmel, picked up two rolls of film, took them out of their boxes, then drove to Long's Drug Store and filled out an order form using the name John Reid.

I handed the form and the rolls of film to the clerk, a short, dark-haired girl who looked bored with the world.

"I'd like these as soon as possible, please. And I have a few rolls ready to be picked up."

She looked at the name on the order slip, went to a drawer, and pulled out three envelopes. "That'll be twenty-six forty, Mr. Reid."

11

Back in the parking lot, I got in the car and started flipping through the pictures. There were several shots of Vanilla in a two-piece micro-bathing suit, looking as exotic as anything to have graced *Sports Illustrated* in recent memory. She was lying in the shade by a kidney-shaped swimming pool. A few pictures showed Slate floating in the pool in an inflatable chair, one hand waving at the camera, the other wrapped around a can of beer. Over a dozen pictures showed Slate and Vanilla in a house, still in their swimsuits, with a group of smiling people, most of them holding glasses and with a heavy-lidded, intoxicated look about their eyes. The others were all dressed in shorts and looked as if they just came from the golf course or tennis courts, except for one tall guy in a sport coat, standing in the background, both hands resting on the back of a wooden chair, a serious look on his face. Bingo. Tom Dykstra himself.

I checked through the other photos again, but there were no other shots of Dykstra.

There were five more pictures. They showed a large iron gate, a high pyrocanthia hedge. The hedge and surrounding trees all looked damp. There was just a glimpse of a house with a gabled roof in the background of two of the pictures. While the shots of the pool and party had a warm, sunny, Palm Springs atmosphere, the others definitely had a cold, wet look. Pebble Beach.

I wasted three hours driving slowly around Pebble Beach, hoping to find an iron gate resembling the one in Slate's pictures. All I had to show for my efforts was a headache.

I drove back to Carmel and found a small real estate office, Dutil Properties. A tall, balding, distinguished-looking man with a neatly trimmed mustache was sitting behind a busy-looking desk, reading a newspaper.

I introduced myself and showed him the pictures of the hedges and gate.

"Ah, the old John Sparrow estate," the agent said after looking at the photographs. "I'm afraid you're too late, young man. Sold over a year ago." He sighed wistfully. "I wish I was involved. Went for a fortune."

"You mean you actually recognize the house?" I asked.

"Certainly. I showed it a number of times. None of my clients had the financing. Some Greek chap ended up with it."

"You're sure it's the same house, Mr.—"

"Dutil," he said, handing me his card, then whisking out a chair with the finesse of a butler. "Sit down. I'm sure there are some other properties available that will interest you."

"The house in the pictures. Could you tell me the address?"

"Ah, excuse me for asking, but are you actually in the market for a home?"

"No, but I'm interested in learning all I can about this particular piece of property."

Dutil slumped back in his chair with the air of a man who was through for the day. "The best address I can give you is Bristol Curve and Lisbon Lane. It used to be called Sparrow's Nest. Strange, isn't it? All these multimillion-dollar homes with cute little names like Lyon's Den, or Cap's Corner. I think I still may have the multiple-listing file on the house."

He went over to an oak filing cabinet and came back with a manila folder. He thumbed through several pages, then handed me the folder. "There it is," he said.

There it was indeed. There were several grainy copies of photographs. The house looked like something out of an MGM musical, where all the rich folk had breakfast in their tuxedos. The house itself was huge. The beautiful gabled roof had four chimneys poking out of it.

The grounds—you'd have to call them grounds, not just a plain old lawn—had the obligatory pool. Not quite big enough to launch an ocean liner in, but it would certainly do. Another picture showed the putting green. Alongside the green were several sand traps and a sunken hot tub. That way if you got tired of blasting the blasted ball out of the sand, you could just flop in the tub and relax. Rich is better was an understatement.

"Can you tell me anything about this Greek fellow who bought the house?"

89

"Sorry," Dutil said with little enthusiasm now that there was no possibility of a sale. "Fantastic place though. Three floors, thirty-six rooms, Italian and Belgian travertine marble throughout. Beautiful grounds: formal garden, swimming pool, even has its own driving range and putting greens."

I drove back to Pebble Beach. The auto and pedestrian traffic was picking up for the golf tournament. I found the house this time. I had probably passed by it half a dozen times earlier but missed it. The gate was set well back from the road, camouflaged by a variety of stately trees and a clump of oleanders.

I parked on Lisbon Lane and walked back to the gate. It was at least ten feet high, a damp, rusting iron filigree that allowed a good look into the property beyond. A large outdoor floodlight hovered from a tree on the other side of the gate. It looked big enough to brighten up the whole gate area at night. I could make out a gravel road that curved lazily for fifty yards, then disappeared into a forest of pines. Just as in Slate's pictures, I could see the tip of a gabled roof. There was an iron post, with a call box to connect you to the house, and one of those slots for a coded plastic card that operates a machine to open the gates. I tried my Bank Americard, but nothing happened. At least I didn't hear an alarm. I checked the gate out but couldn't find any semblance of an alarm system. The one thing that was missing from Slate's pictures was the dogs. I shook the gate a few more times and could hear distant barking. Then they came, a matched pair of powerful-looking Rottweilers. They pounded up toward the gate, and I backpedaled faster than a defensive back covering one of those world-class sprinting wide receivers.

It was too late to check with the assessor's office

to see just who owned the house. I drove back to Slate's place. Still no Vanilla. I called Lieutenant Shroyer's office. He answered and was in his usual grumpy mood.

"What do you want, Polo?"

"Vanilla Hale took off this morning, supposedly to look into a modeling job. I haven't heard from her all day."

"What do you want me to do? Put out an all-points bulletin just because you're alone and horny?"

"I just thought you might have heard from her."

"No. Not since last night, when both of you took off in a hurry. What's really bothering you, Polo?"

"I'm just cooperating, Lieutenant. I thought you might want to do the same. Has Burke told you about the manuscript?"

"What manuscript?" Shroyer's voice rasped irritably.

"I found the manuscript Slate was working on. It was in his golf bag at Pebble Beach."

"Shit" was all Shroyer said.

We waited each other out for what seemed almost a full minute, then he said, "Burke didn't call me. Does he have the manuscript now?"

"He probably has a copy. I called my client. He sent a messenger down from San Francisco. Gilleran was going to make a copy available to Burke."

Another long pause, then: "Did you happen to read this thing before you handed it over to your client?"

"Yes. Not much in it that would help in your investigation of the plane crash. No mention of Dykstra in the book at all."

Shroyer's voice became almost a whisper. "Okay, Polo. Thanks. Since you're cooperating, I'll give you a lit-

91

tle something. That bastard Burke hasn't given me anything, but Wallace, the Secret Service guy, has been
playing ball. Seems the rumor around is that Tom Dykstra
was getting ready to write his own book. *My Life in the
Secret Service,* that kind of shit."

"Did Wallace say that they found the book, or any of
Dykstra's notes?"

"No. Not a page had turned up. So maybe now we
know why Dykstra and Slate were so chummy, huh? Let
me know when the girl turns up."

12

I killed a couple of hours at the Carmel library going through a dozen books on Iran in the days of the shah. Good old Sedez Zadar got a mention as the chief interrogator for SAVAK. Seems one of his favorite methods of interrogation was to have a man beaten half to death, then forced to watch as a chained and muzzled bear raped his wife or daughter.

There was a semiblurred picture showing the shah in one of his comic opera uniforms passing out medals to a group of dark, heavily bearded men in uniforms. One was identified as Zadar. He looked tall compared to the shah, well over six feet, with a large hooked nose, bushy eyebrows, and a heavily pockmarked face. What little hair he had was parted just above his ear and combed upward à la Douglas MacArthur.

Vanilla Hale never came back to Slate's house that night. I spent the evening going back over Slate's manuscript and flicking the TV dial.

By eight the next morning I was in Salinas, the county seat for Monterey County. Salinas is Spanish for "salt marshes," and is chiefly known for producing a large share of the world's lettuce and a big, annual rodeo. It's only some twenty or so miles from Carmel, but the two towns are as different as tacos and crêpes Suzette.

The assessor's office is located in a block of buildings housing the courts and county clerk's offices.

It took some time to pin down the right piece of property. I had to dig through the map books first, then get the right block and lot. But after putting half a dozen green microfiche files into the viewer, I found what I was looking for. The old Sparrow's Nest, as the real estate agent Dutil called it, had been sold by the Sparrow estate over a year ago to a Mr. Nicholas Theodopoulos. Now there was a mouthful. I checked Theodopoulos through the assessor's alphabetical index, but the place in Pebble Beach was the only one he owned in Monterey County.

One was enough. Judging by the taxes, thirty thousand a year, old Theo had put out around three million for the place.

I ran Theodopoulos through more microfiche files: the registrar of voters, the superior, muni and small claims indexes, and met with, as I say in my reports to clients, "complete negative results." Attorneys talk like that, so when you write to them you have to speak their language.

So at least I had a name. But not much more. I used a phone and checked with information, but there was no listing for Theodopoulos. I went out and found a newspaper stand, bought a paper and went through the sports page. There he was all right, Nicholas Theodopoulos, amateur partner of a pro named Jack Voelker. They were scheduled to play at Spyglass Hill, at the start of the tournament, tomorrow, at 10:42 A.M.

I gassed the car up and headed up to San Francisco.

There was nothing much waiting for me at my flat in North Beach other than the usual amount of junk mail and bills. If you're into junk mail, by all means open up a private investigating agency. I mean, we really get the cream of the crop. Catalogs featuring all the latest in electronic devices: bugs, bug detectors, antibug detectors, wiretaps, wiretap detectors, exploding briefcases, lock-picking tools, night-vision binoculars, crossbows, blowguns, flashlights that shoot darts, bullets, or mace. Throwing knives, knives that look like pens or pop out of the heel of your shoe. Flame guns, sword canes. Books on how to turn semiautomatic rifles into machine guns. Books on how to make silencers, bombs, poisons. I'm telling you, there is something for absolutely everyone on your Christmas list somewhere in that junk mail.

Luckily, I had saved a few of the catalogs, and after stopping to admire the pictures of the lady wearing the latest in bulletproof vests, I found what I needed.

Tranquilizer guns. There were two models listed, a rifle and a pistol. The pistol looked like a big BB gun, and was powered by a CO_2 cartridge. The supplier was right in San Francisco, on Folsom Street. I called and was assured by the clerk that they had the gun in stock.

"Would I need a permit for it?" I asked.

"No, sir. What do you intend to use it for?"

"I have a ranch up in Sonoma. There have been a couple of dogs bothering my sheep. I don't want to kill them, but I would like to put them out and take them to the pound."

"Sure, no problem. How big are the dogs we are talking about?" he asked.

"Good-size Rottweilers."

95

"I'd suggest our model XT forty-six syringe for that size animal, sir."

Who was I to argue? I told him I'd be over in a couple of hours to pick up the gun and syringes.

I put the espresso machine on and got down to the main purpose of my visit back to the city: my computer.

I put the proper disk in the proper slot and in no time was connected to a data base in southern California. I fed in the name Nicholas Theodopoulos and, using the right codes, requested information on any property he owned in the state of California, and if he had any civil suits filed in the state.

The computer screen advised me that the request was being processed and the information would be available in an hour.

Next I called a contact at the phone company, and asked for the number for Theodopoulos's place in Pebble Beach. It's harder to get the numbers since they've broken up that old Mother Bell of ours. Even the police have to go through a hassle to get the damn things. Years ago the FBI actually had to come begging to the local cops to get unlisteds because of the stink Bobby Kennedy made by tapping lines in Nevada. Seems the boys that were skimming the casinos found out about the taps, didn't pester the feds, but had a smart attorney who sued the phone company for setting up the tapped lines. Now the cops are having the same troubles, so they either have to put in their requests and wait while they are reviewed by the local phone company for approval or, in a pinch, come to someone like me. If you don't have a contact for unlisted telephone numbers in this racket, you should turn in your trench coat.

My contact stated she'd have the information in half an hour. She also stated that she would be expecting either cash or a money order in her mail box shortly. The underground economy at its best.

I took a shower, packed a suitcase with some fresh shirts, underwear, and Carmel-type sportswear. You can go anywhere in Carmel or Pebble Beach in a camel-haired coat and turtleneck and look like you belong. I also packed an Eddie Bauer mackinaw with half a dozen Velcro-rimmed pockets, and, since I was dealing with the big boys, a .357 Magnum. Then I made an omelet, caught up on the local gossip in the last few days' newspapers, and, when I put the faithful IBM back to work, sure enough, the information was on line.

Mr. Theodopoulos had not bothered suing or was not being sued by anyone in our fair state.

He owned two separate pieces of property, the one I already knew about in Pebble Beach and one in La Quinta, just outside of Palm Springs. Things were getting interesting.

I called the Hall of Justice and caught Inspector Paul Paulsen at his desk.

"Paul, I need a favor. A quick DMV check on a guy." I gave him Theodopoulos's name. That's one thing the police department's computer system has over mine. They can pick up driver's license records and criminal records, even without the party's license number, date of birth, or social security number.

Paulsen was back on the line in little more than a minute. "Your boy shows two addresses, Nick. Both postal boxes, one in Palm Springs and another in Carmel."

"What's his physical description?"

"Six two, two hundred thirty pounds, brown eyes, brown hair."

"Any cars registered to him?"

"Shit," Paulsen said. "You want it all, don't you? Hang on."

This time I had to wait almost five minutes.

"Have you got a lot of ink in your pen?" Paulsen asked when he came on the line.

"Why?"

"Mr. Theodopoulos owns a total of nineteen vehicles, ranging from a 1929 Packard to this year's Corvette. In between there are a few Porsches, a couple of Mercedeses, a BMW, a Rolls, and some more oldies, an Alfa Romeo, a Bugatti, a sixty-four Mustang—you name it. The guy must have his own antique car showroom."

I thanked Paulsen and asked him to mail me the printout, then called the phone company and got Theodopoulos's number.

I called. The phone was answered by a deep male voice. Just one word. "Yes."

I punched out seven numbers on the phone and waited. And waited. Nothing. I punched out the numbers again. The phone was slammed down hard enough to make me pull the receiver away from my ear.

I tried calling again. Busy. I tried twice more. Still nothing but the busy signal.

I picked up my suitcase, and thought I had made a successful breakout, but got stopped on the stairs by my one and only tenant, Mrs. Damonte, a five-foot dynamo who had passed her seventieth birthday when I was still in school.

I was led into her flat and lectured, in Italian, on the facts of inflation, and the rising costs of living, and the neglect of the federal government in taking care of the elderly. This was all leading up to her monthly request for a drop in her rent. Since she was already paying about fifteen hundred a month less than I could get for the place on the open market, I wasn't very sympathetic.

Deep down I knew Mrs. D had a plan. She was going to outlive me. And I wouldn't bet against her. She had been a little heavier than usual on the inflation bit. Maybe they had upped the price of tickets at the bingo parlors.

I made one stop to pick up the tranquilizer gun and got some detailed instructions on its operation.

"Load it, point it, and pull the trigger," the sales-clerk said.

He showed me how to insert the CO_2 cartridge in the pistol's handle and how to load the tranquilizing darts into the barrel.

"You said the dogs were Rottweilers, didn't you, sir?"

"Yep. Big ones."

He placed two boxes of darts onto the table. "The red ones, XT forty-sixes should handle the dogs nicely. You go any bigger than that and you risk killing the animal."

"How long does it take the tranquilizer to take effect?" I asked, remembering scenes on TV of Marlin Perkins and his khaki-clad buddies shooting elephants and lions and carting them off to some safer habitats.

"Shouldn't take more than thirty seconds or so, and should last a good hour or so." He scratched his chin with his fingers. "You're just about on the border with dogs that size. You might want to take a box of these," he said, shaking out some yellow-tipped darts out of a box. They were nasty-looking things, aluminum cylinders about an inch long, with a needle sticking out of one end, the tail a twisted clump of yellow twine. "These are used mostly for small game: squirrels, rabbits, that kind of thing. If

XT forty-sixes don't do the job, another shot with one of these should, without doing any harm to the dogs."

I certainly didn't want to do any harm to the dogs, and I just as certainly didn't want them doing any harm to me, so before leaving the city I stopped at a pet supply shop and picked up two strong and sturdy leather muzzles.

13

It was almost five when I got back to Carmel. There was still no sign of Vanilla. She was a big girl, and it was none of my business what she did with her time, but I had a bad feeling in my gut, which no amount of Alka-Seltzer could cure, that she was in trouble.

Wednesday night is the biggest party night of the golf tournament. They still call it the Clambake, after Crosby's first tournaments when that's just what they had to celebrate, baked clams and lots of booze. Now it's a little more sophisticated. There are two parties really, one for the women guests at the Del Monte Hyatt and one for the men at the Double Tree Inn in Monterey.

I suited up in a camel-hair sport coat, yellow turtleneck, brown Dak slacks, and loafers with tassels. With this disguise I could blend in with the rich and famous.

I slipped Slate's invitation to the Clambake into my pocket, where it nestled against the Beretta, and drove into Monterey. The Double Tree Inn was one of the newer spots in Monterey, down by Fisherman's Wharf, with the usual cluster of shops and boutiques scattered near the lobby. I handed my invitation to a happy-looking guy with a long, narrow nose and a guardsman mustache. He took the beautifully engraved envelope without even looking at it, handed me a blank name-tag sticker, and said, "Have a good time, pal."

Everyone seemed to be having a good time. There must have been over two hundred men, of varying ages and in various states of sobriety, milling around. I wended my way through cashmere sport coats and tartan plaid slacks to the bar and got a scotch over. The bar scotch was Chivas Regal. I took an appreciative sip. A man could get used to this life.

Everyone was clustered in small groups, and all the conversations had to do with bogeys, birdies, and "that fucking wind coming in off the ocean."

I moved around eyeing name tags. Clint Eastwood was hunched over a small table in serious discussion with two guys who looked like bankers even in their checkered pants and alpaca sweaters. Jack Nicklaus was surrounded by middle-aged, potbellied men, who stared at him with all the zeal of their teenage daughters gazing at the latest rock star. No sign of Theodopoulos. I asked around for the young pro that Theo was hooked up with, Jack Voelker, and finally found him leaning against the end of the bar.

He looked to be in his early twenties, with a neat, compact build. He was wearing light-blue pants, a light-blue turtleneck under a dark-blue sweater. The sweater had the name "Amana" stitched over his heart and "Reebok" on the sleeve. There was something stitched just over his right pants pocket that I couldn't read. The kid was a walking billboard.

I held out a hand and he gave me a cautious smile.

"You're Jack Voelker, aren't you?" I asked.

"Yep."

"I watched you on the practice tee. You looked great."

He laughed thinly. "Good thing you didn't see me on the putting green. I made trombones today."

He saw my puzzled look.

"Trombones. That means I shot a seventy-six, you know, like the song, 'Seventy-six Trombones'?"

"Oh, yeah. How's your amateur partner? I don't see him around."

Voelker's features turned wary. "You a friend of his?"

"Do you think he has any real friends?"

His features softened. "Just what do you do, Mr. . . ."

"Harris. I'm in commodities. I have to deal with Theodopoulos, but it's not always a pleasure. All of my contact with him has been over the phone, so I don't really know what he looks like."

Voelker stood on his toes and craned his neck. "There he is, over by the fireplace. Big guy in the camel-hair sport coat doing all the talking."

I looked toward the fireplace. There were four men bunched together. One was taller. A full head of dark hair and a neatly trimmed Clark Gable–style mustache.

"That's Theodopoulos? The guy with the mustache?"

"That's the man, partner. Good luck. You may need it."

I got a refill on my scotch and walked over to where Theodopoulos was holding court. He was a big, big man. Not just tall, but with massive shoulders. Stocky, but it was a good guess there wasn't much fat under his tailored clothing.

He was making gestures with his hands, his dark eyes darting back and forth between his audience. I just caught the punchline of his joke as I got close.

"The one with two eye patches."

The others laughed politely, but Theodopoulos roared at his own joke. It was a deep, cackling laugh that seemed to start at his toes and work its way up.

I stood to one side and looked at his profile. The nose was straight and true, the skin, a healthy tan color, with no sign of any pockmarks. His dark hair had obviously been styled and sprayed, but it covered most of his head. He couldn't have looked much less like the man identified as Zadar in the book at the library.

I felt as if the air had been let out of my balloon. If Theodopoulos wasn't Zadar, then why the hell was Slate so interested in his house? Hell, maybe he just wanted to buy the damn thing, and all I was doing was spinning my wheels.

Theodopoulos must have told another joke, because all of a sudden there was that huge, ugly laugh again.

Well, I could forget it, get loaded and enjoy a free dinner, spend a lot of time following Theodopoulos around, or give it a heavy shot right now and see what happened.

I tapped the gentleman standing nearest to Theodopoulos and asked, "Have any of you guys seen Zadar?"

Theodopoulos's dark eyes narrowed and his facial muscles tightened. Two deep clefts formed between his dark eyebrows. I could almost hear the beads of sweat popping out under his mustache.

"Who did you say you were looking for, buddy?" asked the man whose shoulder I tapped.

"Radar. Radar Harris. I thought he was here a minute ago," I said, in what I hoped was an alcohol-pronounced lisp.

"Never heard of him."

Neither had any of the others. Theodopoulos just bore those mean-looking eyes into me. I got the impression he would never forget what I looked like.

I made my way back to the bar, elbowed my way through the thickening crowd, and got a much-needed refill.

I had hit a bull's-eye with Theodopoulos. The name Zadar had almost dropped him to the floor. A dead-on bull's-eye. I sipped at the scotch and wondered what the hell I was going to do next.

14

A tall, well-built guy in his thirties wearing a dark-blue sport coat and a regimental striped tie nudged my elbow.

"Did you find your friend?" he asked.

I did my best impression, looking stupid. "Friend?"

"That Radar chap you were asking about. I know a man that goes by that nickname. Could be the same fellow."

"Chap." "Fellow." He used words right out of an English drawing room, but the accent was back east, Boston way, or the Cape. His face was rawboned, all hard lines and sharp angles. His dark wavy hair was parted with a razor slash. He held a drink in one hand, but his eyes were dark and sober and staring straight into mine.

"Could be," I agreed. "If his last name is Harris. Fat guy, sells insurance, lives in Los Angeles."

"'Fraid not. My man's Hampton, in real estate. Are you up here to play in the tournament?"

He wasn't wearing a name tag on that beautifully tailored blazer. "No, just a watcher, Mr.—"

He switched his drink to his left hand and gave me a squeeze to show how strong he was. And he was.

"Taylor's, the name, Bill Taylor. And yours?"

"Reid. John Reid."

The name did nothing for him. He was probably too young to have been a Lone Ranger fan.

There was an announcement that the entertainment was about to begin.

Taylor gave me a brief nod and moved out with the crowd. I had enough entertainment for the night so I left and got my car.

I made a quick stop at Slate's house. No sign of Vanilla. I changed into Levi's and the Eddie Bauer mackinaw, whose many pockets I began filling with the Magnum and the tranquilizer gun. I took three of the red-tipped syringes and three of the yellow. If those weren't enough for the dogs, I was calling the escapade off. I took a flashlight, a small crowbar, and my Swiss Army knife, picked up the dog muzzles and headed into Pebble Beach. The entertainment and dinner should keep Theodopoulos away from home for another couple of hours.

I paid my entrance fee to the ranger at the Carmel gate and drove through the darkened Del Monte Forest. I maneuvered the car into a clump of shrubs a good two hundred yards from Theodopoulos's front gate and made my way cautiously along a graveled road. The shrubs covering the wall on this side of his property were a dense and thorny pyrocanthia. I tried wriggling through at a few spots, but it was too thick.

That left me with the gate. The flood light I had seen on my earlier visit seemed overly bright and illuminated all of the gate and a dozen or so yards on each side of it. Time for a little target practice. I loaded a yellow-tipped syringe into the tranquilizer pistol, careful not to prick my finger with the damn thing. I aimed at the light. There was a soft plopping noise as the CO_2 ejected the cartridge. The syringe made a direct hit on the light. There was the breaking sound of glass, then blessed darkness. Then the sound of barking dogs.

I melted back into the darkness and waited. If the light was hooked up to an alarm system, someone from the house should be down to investigate pretty quickly.

The dogs came very quickly. There were two of them again. But no one else came. They barked for a good couple of minutes, then wandered off. I waited ten minutes and walked back to the gate. The dogs couldn't have been far away. They came charging up, teeth bared, ears pinned back.

I didn't feel very good about it, but I started loading the tranquilizer gun. The other dog seemed surprised when his comrade went down after the first shot. I reloaded again, hit the second dog, and waited.

Both dogs were on the ground and out in less than a minute. I always considered myself an animal lover, dogs in particular, but once I was literally almost eaten alive by a Doberman, under the willing command of his master, and ever since I've treated dogs, especially big dogs, with a great deal of respect and plain old fear.

From what I knew of Rottweilers, they were an ancient breed that came to Germany with the conquering Roman armies. Great watch dogs. Big, tough, and loyal. I scrambled over the gate, the intricate iron scrolling making the climb relatively easy.

The dogs were both still. I touched the chest of one. There was a strong, steady beat. I pulled the knockout syringes out, tossed them over the fence, then took out the muzzles and fitted them over the dogs' heads. I didn't know how long those tranquilizers would work, and I sure as hell didn't want the animals waking up grouchy and finding me traipsing around the grounds.

I dragged the two dogs over toward the hedge, then reloaded the tranquilizer gun with another red syringe, just in case there was one more dog lurking about, and started up toward the house. Once I got past the curve in the road, the full size of the building came into view. It was impressive: two stories of slate or stone, with that beautiful tiled roof. The outside was lit with a series of spotlights. Several of the downstairs rooms had lights on. I leaned against an oak tree and watched and listened. No movement from within the house. No noises, other than my own heartbeat, which sounded loud enough to me to be heard back in Monterey.

The front gate wasn't wired, but would the house be left that unguarded? Not likely.

There was a small building set away from the house. I walked over slowly, trying to be as quiet as I could. I remembered reading something about Indians, who were able to move around silently when walking by putting down their toes first, then their heels. I tried a couple of steps that way and almost fell down. Score one for Tonto, zero for the Lone Ranger.

This building was constructed in the same general style as the main house, but was no more than twenty feet high. There were six double doors, all at least twelve feet high and ten feet across. I moved up close to the wall and again stopped to listen, and again heard nothing unusual. But what would be unusual? I asked myself. To hear nothing would be unusual, stupid, I heard the left side of my brain telling the right side. There should be *some* noise—a watchman, a cook, a maid, a housekeeper. A radio or TV playing, the banging of pots and pans. Maybe Theodopoulos ran a tight ship. No stay-over help. But to keep this place in shape there would have to be an army of domestic help during the day. Which was why I was here in the night, the right side of my brain responded smugly to that know-it-all left side.

One of the doors was opened a crack. I opened it a little farther, millimeter by millimeter. No alarms, no more dogs. I slipped inside and turned on the flashlight, the beam stabbing through the dark and imprinting a full moon on the far wall. It was a garage. But not just your average garage. I played the flashlight quickly back and forth. There must have been over a dozen cars. I adjusted the flashlight beam so it was just a pinpoint and checked them over. Dream cars: Porsches, a Rolls, and one bottle-green four-door Packard convertible with huge whitewalls that must have cost more than I'd made so far during my entire life. I was like a kid in a candy store for a minute, until I remembered I wasn't supposed to be there, and the candy store owner might be one very bad dude.

I walked down toward the end of the garage, still bouncing the flashlight off the cars, until I came to the end and skidded to a halt. There was a small light-blue Jaguar parked behind a sleek silver Porsche. Unlike all the other cars I'd seen, this one was not spotlessly clean and polished. It was dirty and battered, the top ripped. It was Slate's car, and when I last saw it, Vanilla Hale was driving it.

The left side and right side of my brain went at each

other again. So, the car was here, what did that mean? That Vanilla was somewhere around too. Probably in the house. Was she a willing guest or not? Why hadn't she called? Because she's a big girl, who doesn't owe you anything, and Theodopoulos probably owned a few magazines and could use a beautiful model like Vanilla on their covers. Maybe she just left the damn car here and flew off to New York, or Mexico, or Paris on a modeling job. All possible. But I really didn't believe it. Which left me with two alternatives. Try to get a look inside the house and see if she was there, or get out as fast as I could and tell Shroyer about the car. Let him tackle Theodopoulos. That seemed like the smart and safe thing to do. But maybe just a peek into the house. Maybe I could— Unfortunately I was prevented from arguing with myself further when someone snapped on the lights.

The whole room blazed under a bank of wall-to-wall fluorescents. I had to blink my eyes, while my right hand reached for the Magnum.

"Don't move an inch, Mr. Polo," someone said in an authoritative tone. An authoritative tone with a Boston accent.

I squinted to the far end of the room. The man who had identified himself as Bill Taylor at the clambake was walking confidently toward me. He could afford to look confident. He was holding a rifle in his hands. As he got close I saw that it had a small crank screwed to the trigger guard.

Thanks to those catalogs I mentioned earlier, I knew exactly what the crank was for. Simple little gadget, called the Activator. Attaches with two set screws to a semi-automatic rifle, then you don't have to bother pulling the trigger. Just turn the crank and every revolution fires off four bullets. If you practice a lot, and you've got a large

111

enough clip of cartridges, you can start churning out twenty rounds a second. Which puts it right up there with a machine gun. His clip reached halfway to the floor. Nice thing about the Activator is that it's legal and has the full blessing of the Federal Bureau of Alcohol, Tobacco and Firearms. And why not? Surely no one would think of doing anything naughty with the damn thing.

Well, maybe Taylor would, though he seemed to be in a happy mood, smiling from ear to ear.

"Really, Polo," he said as he got close enough to nudge me with the rifle barrel. "You are rather clumsy, though that thing with the dogs wasn't bad." He waved the barrel. "Drop the flashlight, and do it very slowly and very carefully."

I followed his orders, then asked, "Why'd you leave the party? Entertainment no good?"

"Back off."

I shuffled backward until I bumped into a car.

"Watch the paint, Polo. And do keep those hands up.

"Yes, not too bad at all. I'm afraid I'm going to have to ask you take off that jacket. Very slowly."

I slipped off the mackinaw.

"Throw it over here," he said. "By my feet, and if you throw it even the slightest bit too hard, or off target, I'm going to take great pleasure in blowing your head off."

I followed his directions. He bent down, picked up the jacket, and took out the tranquilizer gun.

"You've been a busy little man the last couple of days, Polo. I've been keeping an eye on you. Now lie down on the floor, facedown."

I started to protest and the good humor left his voice. "Now!"

I dropped to the floor. It was cement, painted a glossy gray.

"It really wasn't very bright of you breaking in here like this, Polo. It gives me the perfect right to shoot you right now as a prowler."

"The police know I'm here. Besides, the gate was open."

Out of the corner of my eye I could see him fiddling with the tranquilizer gun.

"I'm afraid you're wrong on both counts, Polo. The gate wasn't open. I've got your entire entrance on video. Amazing the results we get with infrared nowadays. And the police would never condone your breaking and entering like that. Now, outside of being a little headstrong, you seem like a reasonably intelligent chap. Tell me how you tied Theodopoulos to Zadar."

"Zadar? I don't think I—"

Something sharp, probably the toe of his shoe, made a violent contact with my ribs. I screamed out and tried to get up. There were two more kicks. I rolled around groaning for several minutes, then tried sitting up. That got me the butt of the rifle in my shoulder.

"Back on the ground, Polo. Facedown. Now, we can keep this up all night, you know. So don't be a bore. How did you connect Theodopoulos to Zadar?"

"Notes," I said. "Slate had a note with the name Zadar on it."

He nudged me with his toe and I almost jumped a foot into the air. "Just the name Zadar? That still doesn't give me the connection."

"Slate had taken some photographs of this house. I found out who owned it. Theodopoulos. When I saw him tonight and mentioned Zadar's name, he almost jumped out of his skin."

"Photographs? Where are they now?"

"In the mail. To Slate's publisher."

He nudged me with his toe again. A little harder. "You'll have to do better than that. If the photographs were around, the police would have found them."

"Slate put them in to be printed under another name. John Reid. It was a joke with him."

"Joke?"

"John Reid was the Lone Ranger's real name."

"The Lone Ranger. How curious. And just how did you come by this astonishing information that seemed to elude the local police, the FBI, and the Secret Service?"

"Slate had the initials L.R. scribbled next to Zadar's name. I knew he liked to play word games. He had a trivia book in his den. I looked until I found someone with the initials L.R."

"You really are a clever chap, aren't you?"

He paced back and forth for a couple of minutes. I winced inwardly every time he came near me. I'd have to make a move soon. If he got close enough I'd have to try to knock him down with a kick. My eyes swiveled along the garage floor. The only possible weapon in sight was the hubcap on an old maroon sedan, and it looked like Arnold Schwarzenegger would break out in a sweat taking it off. I flexed my hands and feet, trying to get myself ready for whatever came.

"Relax, Mr. Polo. I'm not going to kill you. Yet. Exactly what did you tell Slate's publisher about those pictures?"

"Nothing. I just included them with the note."

"And the pictures were just of this house? Nothing else?"

"No, there were some shots of Slate at his place in Palm Springs. Dykstra, the Secret Service man, was in one of the pictures."

114

"My, my. Complications. Doesn't leave me much choice, does it?"

There was that familiar soft plopping noise and a sudden sharp pain in the back of my neck. I tried struggling to my knees, didn't make it, fell down and rolled over. Taylor was standing over me grinning, the tranquilizer gun in his hand.

15

I woke up in sections. I felt my toes move, then my legs, then my chest. Then I made a real bad decision and tried moving my head. Pain like a knife scraping down from my brain to the base of my spine. My mouth had that cottony, too-many-martinis taste. I shook my head slowly. All that did was give the pain time to travel all the way down to my toes. I then got the bright idea of moving my hands. They wouldn't cooperate. I opened my eyes. One at a time. Neither hurt. I was making some real progress here. I looked around to see where I was. In a garage, on the floor, next to Jack Slate's Jaguar. Everything came back to me: climbing over the gate, the tranquilizer gun, the dogs. God, I hoped the dogs didn't feel as bad as I did. Then Taylor, or whatever the hell his name was. He must have been the one who tied me up. Whoever did knew what he was doing. I was hogtied in a sitting position. My hands were tied behind my back, then the ropes were brought down to my feet and back up around my neck. If I tried moving too much, the knots around my neck would tighten up and I'd strangle myself. This one definitely wasn't in the Boy Scout handbook.

I tried inching forward, and after a few hard minutes must have moved all of two feet when I came to an abrupt stop. The rope had been tied off to something behind me. Which meant I would have to try to turn around to see what it was. Which meant more pain, more pressure on the knots, more tightening on the neck, more gagging. Not exactly a pleasant experience, but I didn't really have anything else to do.

Some ten minutes later I was drenched in my own sweat and had managed to rotate myself about 180 degrees. Now I could see what the rope was tied to. Nothing fancy, just the bumper of the Jaguar. No problem. I was now free to go anywhere I wanted, as long as I dragged the car along with me. I sat there for a while, mumbling, sobbing, and feeling awfully sorry for myself and trying to find a position that would, if not make me comfortable, at least limit the pain. Nothing seemed to work. It dawned on me that there was one thing I hadn't tried. My mouth. I opened it and yelled, "Help." At least that's the word I tried to pronounce. It sounded more like the croaking of a jungle beast that Tarzan was strangling with his bare hands.

I kept at it, and it got a little better. A little louder. It didn't do much good though. No one came, so I went back to feeling sorry for myself.

Someone eventually did come. I don't know how long it took, I kept falling in and out of semi-consciousness. The sound of someone walking, the heels of his shoes making sharp, decisive explosions like the bark of guns as he approached, brought me back to life.

117

I was expecting to see that bastard Taylor with his souped-up rifle, but it was Theodopoulos. He was dressed in a suit and tie, with a raincoat draped over his shoulders like a cape. He stood over me glowering.

I started to say "Please" but didn't get past "Pl," when he grabbed the rope going from my feet to my neck and yanked it up with one hand. I bent like a crossbow, the rope digging into my neck. He started pulling me up and down like a yo-yo. He was shouting, screaming at me in a language I couldn't understand. Finally he let go of the rope and lowered his face to within inches of mine.

"You no-good fucking swine. I wish I had more time to spend with you. I would teach you the real meaning of pain. The real—"

"Enough, Zadar," said a voice from behind Theodopoulos's back.

Theodopoulos pulled his head back a few inches, then spit at me. "I don't have the time I want, you miserable bastard. But believe me, you are going to suffer." He straightened up and turned to Taylor. "Alan, get me a can of gasoline."

"Are you all packed?" Taylor asked him.

"Yes, damn it, now get the gasoline."

"That's all I wanted to know." Taylor crouched down and put the rifle on the floor, then pulled a revolver from his waistband and fired. Theodopoulos staggered back against a car, a look of amazement on his face, his hands clutching at his chest, blood seeping through his fingers. He opened his mouth for a final word, but all that came out was a bubble of blood. Then he fell heavily to the floor.

Taylor dropped the revolver, which I was sure was my Magnum, alongside Theodopoulos, bent over, and quickly went through his pockets, taking out a wallet and a thick manila envelope.

118

He walked over to me, undid his pants belt, then pulled out the buckle. A knife blade about two inches long and an inch thick was attached to the buckle. He sliced through the rope going from my neck to my feet, then went behind me and cut the ropes from my hands. I felt both great relief and even greater pain as I moved my arms around in front of me.

"Get up, Polo. Quickly." Easier said than done. I tried moving, but nothing worked in its proper order. He gave me the toe of his shoes in my ribs, and I made it to my knees, then, hanging onto the sides of the Jaguar, pulled myself up to my feet.

Taylor picked up his rifle and jabbed it at me. "Get moving."

He shepherded me to the far end of the building and outside. The sun was out, and from its position in the sky it was still early morning.

I slowed down a bit and got the rifle butt in the ribs again. "Keep moving."

Keep lurching was more like it. We went in a door that led to an oversized kitchen.

"Through there." Taylor motioned to a door, which led out into a large room, elegantly decorated with gilded period furniture, striped wallpaper, and dozens of potted plants.

"Keep moving," Taylor said.

"I'm trying, damn it," I said.

"You don't have far to go. Keep moving!"

Cheering words. We came to a hallway and a wide stairway. Sunlight poured colored beams through a stained-glass window onto the polished wooden floor.

"Up the stairs."

I was afraid that's what he'd say. I hung onto the banister and made my way up to the second floor. Taylor was right behind me, the barrel of the rifle ready to nudge

119

me along when I slowed down. It would have been a good place to try to jump him, if I had the strength, and if my arms and feet would do what I told them to do. Right now it was as if I were speaking to them in a foreign language.

"Over there, through that door." I followed his directions. It was an all-white bedroom. Sunlight filtered through filmy lace curtains. A canopied four poster stood in the middle of the room, and in the middle of the bed lay Vanilla Hale. She was naked. Her body was covered with bruises and scratches, her face battered and swollen.

I staggered over to her and felt for her pulse. It was weak, but it was there.

I swiveled to face Taylor. He had dropped the rifle and was holding the tranquilizer gun.

"Not my doing, old boy. That was Zadar." He took two steps toward me. I balled my fist for what I hoped was one last swing, then he pulled the trigger and one of those damn knockout darts plunged right into my chest.

The impact knocked me to the bed, and I fell on top of Vanilla. Taylor walked over. He looked like he was moving in slow motion. It was like watching an action sequence in one of those Sam Peckinpaw movies. He glided over and pulled the syringe from my chest. He was standing over me gloating, twirling the syringe around in his gloved hand. I saw that the syringe's tail was yellow, then I passed out.

I heard an explosion when I woke up. There was smoke in the room. I tried getting up, and flopped down to the floor and inhaled the smell of raw gasoline. I crawled over to the door. I could hear a roaring sound. I looked out into the hallway. The smoke was thicker there, and there were flames licking the walls.

The heat was building up with every second. There was another explosion, followed in a few seconds by yet

120

one more. I pulled myself to my feet and started down the hallway, but only got a few feet. There was no possibility of getting out that way. The heat was intense. My skin felt like it was melting.

I shut the door and went back to check on Vanilla. She was still out cold. Heavy smoke was starting to edge its way under the door. I went to the bedroom window and heaved it open. There was a straight two-floor drop to the garden below. A thick hedge of junipers hugged the side of the house, then there was a large expanse of lawn. I went back and tried picking up Vanilla. She was too heavy, so I grabbed her by the arms and dragged her to the window. My eyes were running like a faucet and my hands kept slipping off her cold flesh.

I could hear the crackling of the fire as it was eating its way through the door. I pushed and shoved, until I finally got her feet out the window. I held her by her arms and lowered her as far as I could. When her feet were dangling no more than six or seven feet off the ground, I let go. As soon as I saw her come to a jarring halt in the hedge, I climbed out the window, aimed a little to Vanilla's left, and jumped. The shrub's sharp branches were almost a welcoming kiss as I crashed into the junipers. I waited a minute, gulping in huge drafts of fresh air, then pulled myself free of the hedge, grabbed Vanilla, and dragged her away from the house. There was another explosion, louder than any of the others, and a wave of intense heat washed over my body. I was exhausted and fell to the grass, covering Vanilla's body with my own. Something suddenly blocked out the sun. I raised my head to the sky, trying to focus my still-streaming eyes, then began to laugh as I recognized the monster hovering above.

16

"You got more TV exposure yesterday than Jack Nicklaus did," said Lieutenant Elmer Shroyer.

I wrestled against the stiff hospital sheets trying to get comfortable. "What's that supposed to mean?"

"The Goodyear blimp left the action around the golf course when they saw the fire. They filmed you as you dragged the girl from the house. You're a hero, Polo, congratulations."

"How is Vanilla? All the doctors will tell me is that she is 'stable.'"

"She'll be all right," said Shroyer, easing his lanky frame into a frail-looking aluminum and plastic chair. "She had enough dope in her to keep her high for a week. That's probably why she wasn't hurt when you dropped her out the window. She was dead to the world. Her body was as limp as a rubber duck. She's got a few internal injuries, but they say it's nothing that won't heal with a little time."

122

"Internal injuries?"

Shroyer looked beat. Lines of weariness ran from the corners of his mouth to the wings of his nose. His hair was oily and matted, and he had a full day's stubble on his chin. "Somebody played some pretty rough games with her. So much for the girl. Now about you, we've got good news and bad news."

I played straight man. "Give me the good news first."

"The doc says that you can be out of here tomorrow. Nothing but some scrapes, bruises, and a badly sprained knee. Seems you were floating along drug heaven when you went out the window too."

"What's the bad news? That my Blue Shield isn't going to cover everything?"

Shroyer grabbed the arms of the chair and pulled himself to his feet. "The bad news, wise guy, is that when you're released tomorrow, I'm arresting you for the murder of Mr. Nicholas Theodopoulos."

"Lieutenant, you've got to be kidding. I didn't murder anyone. Calm down and I'll tell you the whole story."

"Not just yet," said James P. Gilleran, standing in the doorway with a bouquet of long-stemmed yellow roses under one hand and a box of See's candy under the other. "If you are planning to arrest my client, Lieutenant, I'd like a few words with him first."

"The only reason he isn't in jail now is that the doctors won't release him until tomorrow," Shroyer said hotly.

Gilleran put the box of candy and the roses down on the bed. "Lieutenant, my client will most probably be seeing his own physician, who may have other ideas as to just when it is feasible for Mr. Polo to be released. Now as to your charges of murder. Just what do you have to substantiate them?"

"Nicholas Theodopoulos was shot with a three fifty-seven S&W revolver. Said revolver was found alongside his body in his garage. Said revolver is licensed to your client. Your client was found on the premises. And in addition to murder there are possible charges of arson. I'm going to—"

"This is all bullshit," I said. "I'll take a lie detector test and a paraffin test. I never fired—"

"Nick, shut up," Gilleran said, in a voice more from a locker room than a court of law. "Lieutenant, I'd like a little time with my client."

"Sure," Shroyer said, stopping at the door. "I'll be right outside."

Gilleran followed Shroyer to the door and closed it behind him. He turned back to me smiling. "Please tell me just what the hell is going on, Polo."

I told him everything. About how I found Theodopoulos's house, how I tied him into being Zadar, and how I got into his house and found Vanilla Hale.

"And this man who shot Theodopoulos, shit, let's call him Zadar from now on. The man who shot Zadar, you saw him at this banquet earlier that night?"

"Right. Just after I brought up Zadar's name in front of him."

"And he said his name was Bill Taylor?"

"That's what he told me," I said. "But just before he shot Zadar, Zadar called him Alan. I was lucky. He shot me with a small tranquilizer dart. It knocked me out for only a short time. Long enough for him to start burning the place down. If he'd used the same darts I did on the dogs, the potent red ones, I probably never would have wakened up in time."

Gilleran had been working on the box of See's candies as we spoke. He popped another chocolate in his mouth. "Fantastic," he said, the words distorted by the chocolate. "You really did a fantastic job, Nick. The publisher is going to love this. I'm going to have someone from their office over to talk to you. Pinning down Zadar like that. Imagine the bastard living in Pebble Beach, of all places. Of course we'll have to get some more information out of the girl. After what you did for her, she should be putty in your hands—" He was interrupted when a young nurse came in with my lunch: a dismal tray of fish sticks, dry coleslaw, Jell-O, and coffee.

Gilleran handed the roses to the nurse and asked her to put them in a vase.

"Take them to Vanilla Hale's room, please," I requested.

Gilleran helped himself to a cup of coffee when she'd gone. He picked up a fish stick, weighing it in his hand as if he were assaying it, then let it drop to the tray. "Would you enjoy a decent meal?"

"Yes, and a decent glass of red wine."

"I'll check with the doctor about the wine. Now, the first thing to do is get Shroyer off your back. Of course lie detectors have no value at all in court, but you're sure you'll have no problem in passing a test on questions of whether or not you shot your gun or were in any way connected to the start of the fire at Zadar's place?"

I crossed my heart. "No problem. I'm just afraid they'll ask some other questions that I might have problems with, like how I got onto the property, and how I figured out that Theodopoulos was Zadar, and why I didn't call them when I did."

He wiped his hand on a napkin to get rid of the fish-stick grease. "There will be no such questions. We'll vol-

125

unteer to take the lie detector test, but I'll limit the questions so they have nothing to do with anything except the murder and arson charges." He plucked another chocolate out of the box. "I'll talk to Shroyer now. The fact that we have given him the murderer of Jack Slate and Dykstra, the fact that the murderer was a notorious assassin and butcher of untold numbers of people, and has been living in luxury under his very nose, should make him a much more reasonable man." He sighed deeply. "I suppose this means we will have to talk to that FBI jerk Burke too, but it can't be helped." He patted my shoulder like a coach congratulating a third stringer on scoring a touchdown. "You really did an amazing job, Nick, just amazing."

What was really amazing was that in less than an hour a tuxedoed waiter wheeled in a trolley. Under the crisp white linen were several metal bowls. The waiter explained the menu as he uncovered the dishes: asparagus with Hollandaise sauce, Cornish game hen in a soy and sherry sauce, Green Goddess salad, and for dessert, pears with zabaglione.

"I would suggest a nice light Gamay beaujolais with this, sir," he said, holding a bottle of Fetzer wine up for my inspection.

"Hell of a good suggestion," I said, reaching for the salad. My stomach was growling so much that it had been hard to keep my hands off the crummy fish sticks.

Gilleran came back as the waiter was pushing his trolley out the door.

"How is the food?" he asked.

"Terrific."

He poured himself a glass of the wine and took a sip, then wrinkled his nose. Gilleran was the kind of guy who enjoyed sending bottles of wine back at restaurants.

"Lieutenant Shroyer will be here in about thirty min-

126

utes with his lie detector expert. They are also going to take a test of both your hands so we can show that you did not fire your gun." He paused. "The tranquilizer gun would not leave any powder traces, would it?"

"Nope. Fired by CO_2, not gunpowder. The test is no problem. Even a surgical scrubbing wouldn't remove all traces of gunpowder if I had fired the gun."

"Yes, I know that."

Hell, he was an attorney. They know everything. After you answer the question for them.

"Mr. Burke will be joining Shroyer. Don't answer any questions you don't want to, and if I interrupt, you shut up, agreed?"

"Agreed."

We spent the time while waiting for Shroyer and Burke in going over my story, patching up bald spots.

The lie detector machine was set up right alongside the bed, and the whole test didn't take more than fifteen minutes.

Things had improved as far as testing someone's hands to see if they'd fired a gun. In the old days you had to cover the subject's hands with thick gobs of paraffin, making almost a glovelike cast. Now, though, the crime lab clerk just used a cotton swab to rub a thin material on the thumb and index finger on both of my hands. It became what he described as "neutron activated." The results were sent to the FBI lab, and even the tiniest amount of powder residue showed up. Burke and Shroyer asked their questions while the technician went about his job. There were some heated moments, but everyone was fairly satisfied with the way things worked out.

Shroyer and Burke had as much interest in what Vanilla Hale had to say as Gilleran did. According to Shroyer, she told him that she had been driving Slate's

Jaguar and something went wrong with the car. She was going to look for a phone to call for help when a Rolls-Royce pulled alongside and offered to give her a lift. She got in the Rolls, was held by one man while another put a needle in her arm. She remembered being assaulted by the man, whose description fit Theodopoulos/Zadar. She told them she didn't know how she got to his house and had never seen or heard of him before he picked her up that night.

Gilleran said, "I take it my client is free to leave when he's released from the hospital tomorrow, gentlemen?"

"Yes, he can leave," Burke said, anxious to get away. The information about Zadar must have been burning a hole in his colon. He walked to the door like a man leaving a funeral. Shroyer was right behind him.

Gilleran leaned against the door frame. "The girl, Nick. She's been lying to you since day one. The police are leaving a guard at her door, but she's not going to talk to the local police or the FBI. You saved her life. She owes you. Get her to talk."

17

Vanilla Hale's dark hair was in direct contrast to her pale, waxy complexion. Her eyes were closed, her breath slow, slightly irregular.

The roses Gilleran had brought for me were the only things in her room not hospital issue.

I sat down next to her and waited. And waited. I got up and stretched, went for coffee and the local papers, and waited some more.

The newspapers gave our adventure second-page attention. The first page was taken up with the important stuff: the golf tournament. They must have cropped the picture on our story from the blimp's TV coverage. It had been blown up so you could barely make out my head looking up. Luckily, my body covered most of Vanilla's, otherwise nobody but the *National Enquirer* would have printed the damn thing.

The story stuck mostly to the fire itself and didn't

identify either Vanilla or me. Theodopoulos was listed as the owner of the property, but the name Zadar didn't show at all.

I went through the papers, then out for more coffee, picking up some magazines and paperbacks, then went back to Vanilla's room.

She came awake with a low moaning sound. I pulled my chair closer to the bed and whispered, "Hi, it's me. Nick."

The eyelids flickered and opened; her eyes were like black holes in that pale face. She smiled slowly, as if the movement hurt, then an arm snaked from under the sheets and nervously went to her hair.

"You should have given me a warning," she said in a weak voice. "I'll bet I look a mess."

"You look fine."

Her hand encircled my wrist. "Liar. But thanks." She propped herself up on one elbow. "They showed me the television film, where you pulled me away from the house. I want to thank you, I—"

"Did they show you the PG or the X-rated version? The cameraman in the blimp got a lot more than he bargained for."

"Nick, really, please. I want to thank you with all my heart." Her eyes started watering and she plopped her head back on the pillow.

"Relax, we've got lots of time to talk about it. Just concentrate on getting well. It's all over now."

The tears came slowly, then rained on and on. "It's not over," she said. "It's never over."

It was a tough two days. For both of us. I was at the hospital all day and into the night. Vanilla would be asleep most of the time. When she woke up, she'd cry and grab

130

my hand between both of hers, then doze off. When she spoke it was short sentences: What time is it? What day is it? Please don't leave me. Never anything about what had happened to her.

I kept the florist busy. The doctors and nurses made frequent visits; the nurses always cheerful, the doctor, the same one who treated me, giving me suspicious looks, and asking "When will that policeman outside be gone?"

Gilleran stopped by the first day, eager for news. A bright young woman from Slate's publisher talked to me for a couple of hours, scribbling notes in shorthand on a yellow foolscap tablet.

I asked her what she thought of Slate's manuscript. She wore a businesslike black skirt and jacket. Her glasses were thick, they looked almost bulletproof. She pushed the glasses to the top of her head and I could see the little bites in the bridge of her nose where the nosepiece had clung.

"Between you and me, Mr. Polo, it's not all that much. A lot of it is a rehash of old news. We really have to work on it. Of course Slate's name will sell almost anything. But when we bring this new Zadar material into it, it'll be sensational."

"I read the manuscript and thought it was pretty hot stuff."

She dropped the glasses back down on her nose. "There was, if you'll excuse the expression after what you've just been through, a lot of smoke and very little fire. I've seen Mr. Slate's other manuscripts, and they always had a lot more detail, the real juicy stuff if you will. We're going to have to work on this one."

Shroyer stopped by. He was as grumpy as ever. He'd never forgive me for not telling him about Zadar sooner.

I drove up to San Francisco to pick up some clothes

131

and a bigger gun. All I had now was the little Beretta. Shroyer still had possession of my Magnum, and he didn't seem in any hurry to let me have it back.

If you want to buy a handgun from a dealer in the state of California, you must go to the store, pay the price, fill out a form giving all your vital statistics and promising that you're not a felon, then the state says you must wait fifteen twenty-four-hour periods before you can pick up the weapon. (Fifteen twenty-four-hour periods means sixteen days, but naturally, the civil servants would never want to make it that simple for us.)

That's how you buy a handgun off a legitimate dealer. If you want the gun right away, you can go to a flea market and find all kinds of not-quite legitimate dealers, and walk away with almost anything smaller than a grenade launcher right away. Or you can buy a used gun from a private party. I didn't have time to fool around at a flea market, so I went to the next best source, a cop. In this case, Chris Sullivan, the range master at the police firing range, out on the foggy shores of Lake Merced. Sullivan was a tall, broad-shouldered man whose face looked a hundred percent Irish, except for a large sweeping nose that belonged in the desert on somebody riding a camel. He was a master gunsmith and a collector of handguns and rifles.

I found him in his office at the range and told him I was in the market for a gun. Preferably a Magnum.

"Three fifty-seven or forty-four?" he asked, walking over to a battered oak chest and opening a drawer. There were dozens of gleaming, well-oiled pistols and revolvers in the drawer.

"Something with stopping power, Chris. Maybe an automatic, with a big clip."

"No automatics," he said firmly. "Never can tell

when they're going to jam, no matter how much you pay for the damn thing. What are you using now?"

"I had a Smith & Wesson three fifty-seven Magnum. All I've got now is a twenty-five Beretta and a thirty-eight snub nose I keep in the car."

"Keep the thirty-eight, dump the Beretta," he said, picking up a long-barreled revolver from the drawer, hefting it in his hand, then swinging the cylinder opening and handing it to me. "Colt Python three fifty-seven, four-inch barrel. It's still as good as anything they make, Nick. Ventilated ribbed barrel, target barrel, hell of a gun."

Like all big guns, it felt like it weighed a ton. "This is fine, Chris, but I still like the Beretta for its lightness." I took the Beretta out of my pocket and flipped open the barrel.

Sullivan took it, pulled out the clip, then pulled back the hammer and quickly and expertly field-stripped the gun. He snorted through that curving nose and tossed the Beretta into a waste can. "An accident waiting to happen," he said. "Damn things always jam, just when you need them." He turned back to his armament chest and pulled out a lower drawer. "You want something light, take this little thirty-two S&W revolver. Just a little bigger than the Beretta, and," he said, pointing a finger as big as a billy club at me, "it won't fucking ever jam."

We settled on a price for the two guns, then Sullivan insisted I try them out on the range before leaving. Both guns seemed fine to me, but Sullivan wasn't satisfied and put molded plastic grips on both of them.

"Better grip, better results," he said, patting my back with a beefy hand.

My answering machine was loaded with calls about my television appearance. Some were from friends and were cheerfully obscene, others from clients visibly impressed and with work for me to do. The mail had a few new cases too. I passed them on to John Henning and Duane Weeks, the only other investigators in town I trust, and, after packing some fresh clothes and having the mandatory chat with my tenant, Mrs. Damonte, I headed back to Monterey.

By the third day Vanilla was sitting up and eating. She was keeping the spoken word to the minimum, but at least the color was coming back to her cheeks. She took a bite out of her evening dessert, orange sherbet.

"I'm looking forward to some real food."

"The doctor says you can check out tomorrow, if you want to."

She slid back down under the covers.

"I'm afraid, Nick. Afraid. It's safe here. I don't want to go out there."

"I'll be with you."

She cocked her head to one side and studied me. "Forever?"

"Some women have complained that a weekend with me seemed like forever."

She laughed. It was good to see her smile and hear her laugh. "I'll make a deal with you, Mr. Polo. You arrange for a beautician to come in here and make me halfway presentable, and we'll try that weekend out."

18

A heavy storm had come in off the Pacific Ocean, bringing strong winds and sheets of rain. The car's windshield wipers swished, carving twin arcs out of the downpour as I pulled away from the hospital parking lot.

"Where are you taking me?" Vanilla Hale asked.

"I booked a suite at the Jade Tree Inn. I thought we'd wait out the storm right here in Carmel. Then we can go somewhere and get some sun. How's that sound?"

She swiveled stiffly and looked behind us.

"Are you afraid we're being followed?" I asked.

She gave me a weak smile.

I drove through Carmel, taking quick lefts and rights, and after a few minutes I was sure we weren't being followed.

I pulled into the Jade Tree Inn's parking lot. Vanilla made sure I parked well off the street, where the car couldn't be seen from the road.

135

I carried her luggage up to our room. I had champagne on ice and a fire roaring in the fireplace, so it was nice and warm and cozy when we got inside. Once the door was closed and I dropped her luggage, Vanilla threw her arms around me. I carried her to the bedroom and we made love slowly, tenderly, each taking extreme care not to aggravate the other's bruises and bandages.

"Now I know what it's going to be like to fuck when I'm eighty," Vanilla said, running her nails down my back.

"We were a little—" I groped for the right word, "cautious, weren't we?"

"Cautious." She laughed. "We damn near needed medical supervision."

"How about a glass of wine?" I asked, reaching for the ice bucket.

"Cheers." Vanilla knocked down most of the drink I gave her in one gulp. I poured some more champagne in her glass, filling it to the brim.

"You trying to get me loaded and take advantage of me, Mister Private Eye?"

"I thought I'd already taken advantage of you."

Her face crumbled in a rueful smile. "Everyone does." She ran a finger around the rim of the wineglass, finding the pitch of resonance.

"We have to talk about it, Vanilla," I said.

"I know, I know. It's just not easy."

"Take your time. Relax. We've got lots of time."

"Do we?" She paused, breathing deeply, composing herself. "I had problems with Jack's old car. It just stopped, and I couldn't get it started. Then this big Rolls came along. There were two guys in the car. They were polite, asked if I needed help, then one of them grabbed me and pulled me into the backseat." She drained her

136

glass, then dug into her purse for a cigarette. "I struggled, but they were too strong. One of them, the driver, stuck a needle in my arm. I woke up in a bedroom sometime later. I don't know how long I was out. They just kept sticking needles in me." She stubbed out the half-smoked cigarette in an ashtray and immediately shook another from the pack. "That's it, except that big bastard was a real pervert. A sick, mean son of a bitch. Did the doctors tell you what kind of drugs they were feeding me?"

"Yes, speedballs. Heroin and cocaine mixed together."

"It's like one drug is pulling you down, while the other pulls you up, and you end up feeling like you're going sideways," she said, running a hand down the inside of her left arm, across the now almost invisible needle marks.

"The men in the car. What did they look like?"

She crossed her arms, hugging herself in a protective gesture. "The one that pulled me into the car was big, real big, dark hair, maybe fifty or so. The other was younger, smaller. I really didn't get too good a look at him."

"Did they both assault you at the house?"

"Yes, the smaller one just once. The big bastard all the time."

"Did you hear them call each other by their names?"

"No. I never heard a name. And I was so full of drugs, I wouldn't have known if they did."

It was the same story she'd told the police.

She held out her glass. "Talking makes me thirsty."

"Did the police mention the name Zadar to you?"

"Over and over. I told them I never heard of the bastard. What is this, Nick? You're as bad as the cops. Are you working for them?"

I reached out and gently touched her bare shoulder.

137

"Both the police and the people from Slate's publisher want me to get you to talk. They don't believe what you're telling them, Vanilla, and frankly, neither do I."

She pulled herself away from me. "So that's the deal. You play nice-nice with me, pump me to see what I'm holding out, and then run to the cops. Great!" She flung her wineglass toward the fireplace and turned over on her stomach, pounding the mattress.

I waited until she calmed down. "Vanilla, I told them I'd talk to you. Nothing more. There's no deal between me and the cops or the publishers. I don't care about them. I do care about you. I'm just trying to help. Believe me."

She turned around and motioned for me to come to her. She put her lips next to my ear and whispered, "Nick, I'm afraid. For both of us. Really afraid."

"Vanilla, don't be—"

She pulled my head down to her lips again. "Shhh, this room may be bugged. You don't know these people. They're different. You can't touch them, but they can get you, or me, so easily."

I lay next to her, cradling her head in my hands. "I won't let them hurt you. Trust me."

She buried her head in my chest, then moved up and whispered into my ear again. "They'll kill us both. If you try to find them, they'll kill us both."

I started to move away, and she pulled me back, the strength in her arms surprising me. "I'm serious," she hissed. "Listen to me. If I tell you the truth, will you promise to keep it just between us? You won't talk to Shroyer, or the FBI, or anyone?"

"I promise. Just between you and me," I said in a hushed tone, the kind I used to use when going to confession.

138

"I don't know who killed Jack Slate. It may have been this Zadar. I was told to get close to Jack, monitor his writing. I—"

"Who ordered you?"

She stiffened against me. "Shhh. Not so loud. I'll come to that. Now just listen. My—my friend wanted to know what Jack was writing about the Shah of Iran. Wanted me to keep him informed. That's all I promised to do. It wasn't hard, and I liked Jack. This Zadar was a big wheel with the shah. Somehow Jack found out he was here in Pebble Beach. I don't know how, but he did. It might have been from Dykstra, the Secret Service guy. It got my friend nervous. That's when he sent someone out to check on things."

"Who came out?" I asked. "From where?"

"Alan Norton. He's kind of a troubleshooter. I told them I wanted out when Jack was killed. Then when I heard about that poor woman, the Secret Service man's wife, I knew it was Norton. And that private investigator, what's his name? The one you found breaking into Jack's house."

"Paul Sanders."

"Yeah, well, when he was found dead, all hell broke loose."

"You were in contact with them all the time, weren't you?"

Her head retreated into her neck, like a turtle's popping back in its shell. "Yes, Nick, I was."

"Why?"

"I had to, damn it," she said. "He's been good to me."

"He? Alan Norton?"

She threw her hands up in the air. "No, no, not that

139

creepy bastard. He's the one that took me to Zadar's house."

"Alan Norton is the man who tried killing me, killing both of us," I said.

"Yes, he's a killer." She shuddered. "A real killer. But he—he—was never supposed to hurt me. Alan acted on his own."

I shook my head. "I'm still not sure just what the hell you're talking about, Vanilla."

"Alan was my control. I reported to him. We had a special signal. He called me, and I went to the meeting place, but he wasn't there. I got scared, so I called him, and he said that he hadn't sent me a signal. Said that I was panicking. He met me and I followed him. He took me Zadar's house."

"This signal of yours, what was it?"

"A series of beeps on the phone. Seven beeps, and I was to meet him at a prearranged place."

"So Alan, your control, took you to Zadar's house."

"Yes. I didn't know who Zadar was then. He and Alan argued about me. Alan wanted to kill me, right then. He had no more use for me, I guess. That other bastard, Zadar, had other things in mind. They both raped me. Then Alan told Zadar that he could have me, 'but don't keep her too long.' Those were his exact words, like I was a piece of meat, and they were going to use me before I spoiled."

I rested my head against her shoulder. "Alan was your control. You make it sound like you're a secret agent. I believe you, but it still doesn't make any sense. Who the hell is behind all of it? Who is your friend? Who was Alan's control? Who cared that much about Slate and Zadar? Who?"

"An—important man, Nick. A good friend of mine."

140

"A good friend? Lady, I'd hate to see what you call an enemy. What are you talking about? What makes a man so important that he can go around killing people and having you hold back his name from the police?"

"You don't understand, Nick, you just don't understand."

"Vanilla, I need more. I need a name. I want to get him off our backs."

She reached down and pulled the sheet up, covering herself to her chin. "No, Nick. You can't."

"I can with your help."

"He promised to leave me—us, alone."

"Promised? When?"

"At the hospital. He called."

I framed my words carefully before replying. "Listen, they fill you full of heroin and cocaine and use your body like it was a throw-away toy, then they try to kill you, would have killed you if I didn't stumble along. Your friend, whoever he is, knows Norton is an animal, but he left you at his mercy. He's not going to stop now because of one phone call." I ran my hand down the side of her face. "I don't know what he has on you, what it was that made you help him in the first place. I don't want to know. But I can help. We can beat them. Trust me."

"Damn it, Nick. You'll never beat him. He's too big, and, and . . . he's been very good to me. This was all a mistake with Alan. I—"

"Good to you, what the hell do you mean?"

Her eyes turned hard. "It's easy for you, isn't it? It's easy for men. I've been working my ass off since I was fourteen. Fourteen, Nick. That's when I got into modeling. It was fun and glamorous then. The good years, between fourteen and twenty-five. After that, it gets to be a

141

little bit more of hell every day. Look at me. I'm thirty-two now. What do you see?"

"I see a beautiful woman in the prime of her life," I said truthfully.

"Hmmmmph!" She snorted. "Prime, bullshit. Every day you wake up and check to see if another wrinkle popped up over night. You examine yourself in the mirror, notice a little sag here, a little blotch there. All the makeup, Retin-A, and exercising in the world won't stop it, Nick. Nothing will. And there are thousands of little bitches out there loving it; sweet, lovely young things, whose long legs haven't a sign of a sag or a vein, with tight little asses and tits that stick straight up and defy the laws of gravity. And they look at you and smile, know that your time has gone and it's their time now. I worked my ass off for years and had nothing to show for it. He—he helped me, Nick. He'll continue to help me. He said that everything would be okay." She reached out a hand to me. "Okay for both of us. You too. Just drop it and you'll be left alone."

I looked into those big eyes and felt a sudden sadness hit me like a wave. Poor, beautiful Vanilla. I wondered how many women—plain, homely, or even those just considered attractive, the ones who worked at boring jobs, raised children, and stuck it out with men they found weren't exactly Prince Charming—I wondered just how much they would have given to look like Vanilla.

"So, this whoever he is, set you up with Jack Slate," I said.

"Yes. It wasn't hard. He made sure I got invited to the right parties. Jack loved flattery. I read all his books, made the right comments at the right time. And I was another trophy for him to hang around his belt. Jack loved making it with actresses or models."

"But why go through all that trouble to get to Slate?"

"The book he was writing. On the shah. They wanted me to monitor it. See just how far he was getting."

"Vanilla, this is crazy. I'm not going to go through life worrying about some asshole named Alan Norton coming along and putting a bullet in my head. Or your head. Do you really think that they'll leave you alone after what's happened?" I put my hand on her chin. "Think about it. You're a liability. Give me a name, or I'll have to go to the police."

"But you promised. You promised you wouldn't. That you just wanted to help me, not the damn police!"

"I do want to help you. I do. But I can't do it by doing nothing. Give me this man's name. I want to make a deal with him. I've got something he wants. A copy of Slate's manuscript and his notes, notes I didn't turn over to the police or publisher. It's something we can deal with. Something that can guarantee our safety. But we've got to call this man. I've got to talk to him."

She struggled to a sitting position, found the champagne and drank directly from the bottle.

"I'm going to need a lot more of this in me before I make that call," she said, shaking the empty champagne bottle.

"Not to worry." I smiled, reaching for another bottle. "When we run out of French, we can switch to the California brands."

19

It wasn't until the following morning that Vanilla agreed to give me a name. Martin Bledsoe.

"Who the hell is Bledsoe?" I asked her over a breakfast of bakery rolls and coffee. She was still too frightened to eat out at a restaurant.

"You never heard of him?"

"Color me stupid, but no. I never heard of the man."

She lit a cigarette, pulling the smoke slowly through her lips and letting it escape just as slowly out her nostrils.

"Martin Bledsoe is a fixer. On a grand scale. He worked a lot with Kissinger at the State Department. The Middle East was his specialty."

Her eyes glazed over, and she stared out the window. The big storm had blown through during the night, but the sky was still gray and threatening.

"Let's give him a call," I said.

144

She took a last drag on her cigarette, then ground it out in the motel's glass ashtray.

"All right. Here goes. I might as well tell you." The telephone prefix was 202, the District of Columbia. She gave me the full number. She said Bledsoe lived in a beautiful old brick house in Georgetown, not far from the White House.

"Okay, now tell me the truth. Is Bledsoe expecting to hear from you?"

She started to pick up her coffee cup, but her hands were shaking too much to hold it. The cup clattered against the saucer when she dropped it back on the table.

"I—I said I would call and let him know how—how everything went with you. What you were going to do."

There are devices not readily available to the public that can run an immediate trace on the phone you're calling from. They're very expensive and difficult to get hold of, but if what Vanilla was telling me was the truth, there was a good chance that Mr. Bledsoe had access to one.

"You call him, but not from here." I picked up the phone book. "I think I messed up all that gorgeous hair of yours. Let's find a beauty salon to do some repair work."

Vanilla got an appointment in a shop in Monterey. I told her it would be a good idea if she had her hairstyle changed, the color lightened. She seemed surprised.

"We'll change our luck. Make a new start."

I wasn't so much interested in how her hair looked, as long as she was tied up in a beauty salon seat without access to a phone.

We checked out of the Jade Tree, then stopped at a phone booth at the Casa Munras in Monterey and Vanilla called Washington, D.C. She kept her eyes on me the whole time she was talking.

145

"This is Vanilla. May I speak to him, please?" she said to whoever answered the phone.

There was a long wait, then she said, "Yes, I'm fine, thank you. He's with me now. He says that he has something that would be of interest to you. Some notes that Jack wrote."

She stared at me without blinking as she listened. "No, he won't tell me. He wants to talk to you himself. He—"

I took the receiver from her. "We'll get back to you." Then I hung up, severing the connection before he had a chance to say anything.

"He's not going to like that," Vanilla said.

"We have to stop worryng about what he'll like and start thinking about what we like."

I dropped her off at the beauty shop. There was a restaurant across the street. I bought a cup of coffee and brought it over to the pay phone, which was by the window, and gave me a view of the beauty shop.

Before calling Bledsoe, I had to make another call, to a gentleman who worked out of his house in Los Angeles and was listed in the Yellow Pages as a "financial analyst." What he analyzes is his unauthorized, illegal computer connections to banks and savings and loans. You want information on a bank account, he is the man to go to. If he'll deal with you. Before you can open an account with him, he runs a check on you only slightly less tight than they do for a nominee to the Supreme Court. If someone doesn't pay his bills on time, that someone suddenly finds his personal bank accounts have been turned upside down. The guy is crooked, ruthless, and vindictive. I love him. We've made each other a lot of money over the years.

He answered the phone with his usual response, a low grunt.

146

"I need information on two gentlemen, and I need it fast," I told him.

"That is what I am in business for, Nicky, but rush orders do cost more."

"I know. Here's what I have. First name: Nicholas Theodopoulos, addresses in Palm Springs and Pebble Beach."

"Do you have his social security number?"

"No."

The grunt again. "Not having it also adds to the cost, my young friend."

"Next, Martin Bledsoe. Lives in Georgetown, District of Columbia. I don't have his social either."

His voice dropped to a confidential whisper. "Well, well, you are moving in high circles, aren't you? I presume we are talking about *the* Martin Bledsoe."

"Big wheeler-dealer. Right. Does that cause any problems?"

"It might make getting the material a little more difficult and thus more expensive."

"Just get it. When can I call you?"

"Tomorrow morning."

I had the feeling that he could put his magic machines to work and have everything I needed in fifteen minutes, and that the stall until tomorrow was just to fatten his fee. But since he was the only one I knew who could get this information, I thanked him and hung up.

Vanilla seemed in good spirits after her visit to the beauty shop. The style was softer, the color a lighter brown, with streaks of blonde. She looked wonderful. We celebrated with a long dinner at a restaurant in Cannery Row.

We spent the night at a motel in Sand City, a little town a few miles north of Monterey, near the Fort Ord army base. I went out and bought breakfast. I used a pay

147

phone again to call my financial wizard. My credit card was taking a hell of a beating.

"Get out your pencil, Nick," he told me.

He started with Theodopoulos's bank records first, reading off the account numbers and the amount of money currently in each account. There was a lot of money parked in six different banks and eleven savings and loans. Theodopoulos/Zadar also had active accounts with Merrill/Lynch and three other stockbrokers.

One of the banks was in Switzerland, and there were a lot of transfers shuffled through it.

Bledsoe's records were even more detailed than Theodopoulos's, and included banks and savings and loans in America, France, Brazil, Hong Kong, and that old favorite, Switzerland, again.

"The Swiss banks. Do they still have those famous secret numbered accounts that no one but the owner can get into?"

"Certainly, that's what keeps the Swiss in chocolate and gold watches, but the gnomes of Geneva have softened up a bit of late. Both France and the United States have been able to obtain information from the accounts, but only after lengthy court battles. Of course they had to prove that the monies in the accounts came from illegal sources. Then there was that thing with Marcos and all that money he took out of the Philippines. Millions were transferred back to Manila. Even though it was just a slight crack in the wall of security, the Swiss weren't at all happy about it."

"Can you get any information from them?"

He sighed. "Regrettably, no."

Both Bledsoe and Theodopoulos had listed accounts in the same Swiss Bank, Credit Suisse. Of course, there was no telling how many other accounts they had under different names.

"How much do I owe you so far?" I asked.

"Two thousand dollars."

Both Bledsoe and Theodopoulos's accounts at Credit Suisse started with the letter *R*.

"Tell me about the Swiss banks. Say I wanted to open a secret account. How would I go about it?"

"Well, some of the banks have branches here in America, but, if we're talking about a lot of money, the safest way would be to travel to Geneva, Switzerland, yourself. Pick your bank, there are dozens of them, identify yourself and simply open the account. There's nothing special about the damn things."

"Except that no one is supposed to be able to get into them except you. Is it like the movies, you make up your own account number, or name?" I said.

"More or less. They require a signature card. You of course pick the name. It could be your real name, a phony name, whatever, and there can be additional instructions: a thumb print, a code word, whatever, but when you come in to get to your cache, the signature had better match. Very methodical, the Swiss. They assign you a number, or letter, or series of numbers to start the account that fits into their bookkeeping system."

"Sort of the bank's code?"

"Well, I guess you could call it a code. It's simply their way of handling the accounts. Of course, you may add on any other numbers or letters you want to personalize it."

"Then I need the name of a Swiss Bank, other than Credit Suisse, and the first letter or numbers they would use on their confidential accounts."

The request produced a small chirrup of a laugh. "Whatever for?"

"I'm running a bluff. I need a little ammunition. Can you do it?"

149

"Nicky, I don't know, that would—"

"Five hundred dollars if you can get it in thirty minutes."

He could, and did. All the Warburg Bank's special accounts started with the letter *L*, number 6. I wondered why the hell that particular letter and number as I made my thanks and promised to have a check in the mail in the next three days, before hanging up.

I made a call to the airport and got the flight schedules from Washington to Los Angeles, then went back to the motel and packed our belongings and took them out to the car while Vanilla ate breakfast.

I used the motel phone this time, and since it was time to give my credit card a rest, called collect.

"Hello, this is the long-distance operator. I have a collect call from Mr. Nick Polo for either Martin Bledsoe or Alan Norton. Will you accept the charges please?"

Whoever answered the phone asked the operator to hold on a moment. It was a long moment. Finally a familiar voice came on the phone.

"Who did you say it was, operator?" he asked.

"Nick Polo."

"Yes, I'll accept the charges."

"Sounds like my old friend Bill Taylor," I said. "Or is it Alan Norton today?"

"You're very stupid to call here, Mr. Polo. I assume you obtained this number from the young lady."

"Right. How's Marty doing? Put him on, I'd like to talk to him."

"Don't push it," he said harshly.

"Careful, Alan old chap. You're losing your accent. I want to talk to Bledsoe. I have something he may be interested in buying."

"The girl? Isn't she awfully used merchandise?"

150

I had to fight to keep my voice calm. "Sure is. But I'm not talking about that merchandise. I'm talking about Slate's manuscript."

"It's already at the publisher's, so again you're trying to sell something that's already past its prime."

"But I bet it would make interesting reading for you and Marty. Might give you a head start in plugging up some holes. When I found the manuscript, there were some notes in it. Interesting stuff. Slate must have gotten some information from his Secret Service connection. There are all kinds of bank account numbers listed. Some under the initial Z, and we know who that is, don't we? And some under the initials MB. Now who do you think that would be, Alan?"

"You're bluffing."

"Tell Marty about it. I'll call back in about half an hour. Tell him I want to talk to him directly."

I hung up before he could respond.

I stopped at a gas station sitting under a billboard of a huge artichoke advising me that I was in Castroville, the artichoke capital of the world, and called Bledsoe again. Collect. Norton answered and accepted the call.

"I want Bledsoe," I said.

"I'm on the line, Mr. Polo." Bledsoe's voice was soft and reasonable. "How can I help you?"

"Well, I'd like a loan. A large loan. Oh, say, two hundred and fifty thousand dollars. I don't want to be in any hurry to pay it off either, Marty."

"And just what is your collateral, sir?"

"I told your man Alan about the manuscript."

"Yes, I'm curious about that. Just where did it turn up?"

151

"In Slate's golf bag at Pebble Beach. Rather stupid of Alan not to think of looking there, wasn't it?"

"A miscalculation, I would have to agree."

"Well, agree to this, Marty baby. The loan I mentioned, in cash, for the manuscript and some notes I'm sure you'll find fascinating. Notes that the publisher doesn't have. Yet."

"How could I be sure that these notes would be valuable, sir?"

"I'll give you a little peek." I read off the numbers of Theodopoulos's accounts in Monterey and Credit Suisse. "Then there are a lot of account numbers under the initials MB. Here's a couple." I gave him the Hong Kong and Switzerland bank and their numbers.

"Oh, there's one more account under Z. Also in Switzerland. I'll call you in an hour or so and see if we've got a deal."

He was hooked. The next calls were from a coffee shop in San Jose. The first to United Airlines reservations, the second to Bledsoe. He answered the phone himself this time.

"I think we should discuss this deal further, Mr. Polo. It interests me."

"United's flight three forty-three leaves Dulles Airport tomorrow morning at nine-twenty and arrives in San Francisco at one-thirty P.M. I've already made reservations in your name. For two. I assume you'll want to bring Alan along."

"You expect me to come out to California?"

He pronounced California as if it were the name of a newly discovered disease.

"The Indians haven't attacked the forts in years, you'll be safe. And tell Alan not to bother blowing up my place in the city. We won't be staying there. I want to live

152

long enough to enjoy that money. You can contact me through my answering machine."

"Alan will come. I hope it will be a worthwhile trip for him. If he thinks it is necessary, then perhaps I'll join you. Tell me, how is Vanilla?" Bledsoe asked.

"She's doing fine."

"I'd like to say a word to her."

"No chance," I said, breaking the connection.

20

We were back in San Francisco a little after one o'clock. I checked into a motel on Lombard Street and spent the rest of the afternoon and early evening lining up private investigators John Henning and Duane Weeks for help at the airport in the morning.

Vanilla was swinging back and forth between highs and lows. She'd either be very up and happy and bubbling with enthusiasm, or down, depressed, and certain that we were going to fail and that we'd both be killed.

We were close enough to walk to Gelco's, the best restaurant in town when it comes to lamb dishes, and the food buoyed her spirits again.

We spent the evening in the motel watching TV and looking at the clock. By eleven the next morning John Henning stopped by to stay with Vanilla, and a little after noon I was at the airport coffee shop with Duane Weeks. Weeks is a dapper man in his fifties, with hair the color and consistency of steel wool. He runs a shop that specializes in surveillance. He had three of his best operatives with him: Gayle Olson, Kathy Dunn, and Gary Bartolotti. We went over the plan. Bartolotti, a tall dark-haired man in his late twenties with a Tom Selleck mustache and profile, would be waiting outside the main terminal in one car. Gayle and Kathy would follow Norton on foot from the gate once I identified him. Both women were young, bright, and attractive, were dressed like successful businesswomen, and blended in well with the commuter passengers who dominated the terminal at that time of the morning.

Weeks would wait outside in another car. Just how Norton decided to get to the city—rent a car, take a taxi or a shuttle bus—would determine how we'd follow him. If he rented a car, Gayle would be right behind him in line and rent one herself, keeping close so we'd get a description of the rental car and, I hoped, the plate. If he took a cab, Kathy would be right behind him, hoping to hear if he called out his destination to the cab driver, then she'd get in a cab herself and get to utter a line I've wanted to say all my life, "Follow that cab."

There are two street levels at San Francisco International Airport, the upper for departing flights, the lower for arriving. The trouble was, you could get a cab or have someone pick you up at either level. Bartolotti would be jockeying his car around on the lower level, Weeks would be doing the same on the upper level. All five of us had walkie-talkies so we could communicate. I think I mentioned earlier how difficult, and expensive, it was to really do a tail job on someone. This was worse, because I was going to have to pay the bill.

The flight schedule showed that United's flight 343 from Washington was on time, and due to arrive at 9:30

A.M., at gate 84. I had a nervous breakfast, and by 9:00 was sitting in one of United's boarding area's by the gate.

I had a newspaper on my lap, ready to pull up to cover the bottom half of my face. A pair of dark glasses and a Giants baseball cap covered the top half. Gayle Olson was sitting alongside me.

When the plane pulled to the gate, she moved two seats away.

Norton must have traveled first class. He was with the first group of four or five that exited into the terminal. He was wearing a blue suit and had a black leather carry-on bag hanging over his shoulder. He kept his eyes pointed down toward the floor.

"That's him, Gayle. Blue suit with the bag over his shoulder." I turned away and walked fifty yards in the opposite direction North had taken.

When I turned around I took the walkie-talkie from my jacket. "Gayle's got him," I said.

Her voice soon came over the speaker. "He's walking straight toward you, Kathy. Blue suit, black luggage, good-looking, just moving around that woman with the stroller."

"Got him."

I loped along slowly, not wanting to catch up with them.

The walkie-talkie emitted a little static, then Kathy's voice came on. "He's taking the escalator down to the lower level."

Then Weeks came on. "Gary, lower level, he'll be yours. I'll wait here, by United arrivals for you, Nick."

"Be right there," I transmitted, picking up speed now.

Kathy's voice came on again just as I got outside and was looking for Weeks's car. "It's a cab. Yellow number

156

six thirty-four. I couldn't hear where he's going. I'm getting into the cab behind him."

I got into Weeks's car, breathing deep and sweating.

Gary Bartolotti's voice transmitted, "Gayle, I'm by the outer curb, behind the shuttle bus, hurry up."

"Glad you don't do a lot of this work, huh, Nick?" Weeks said with a smile on his face.

"Absolutely correct."

It turned out to be absolute overkill. Norton's cab took the boring drive into San Francisco, along the Bayshore Freeway, to the Broadway off-ramp, down Montgomery to Sacramento, a right turn, then another right on Kearny and pulled to a stop in front of the Holiday Inn.

Weeks picked up his walkie-talkie. "He's going into the hotel. Kathy and Gayle, follow him in, see if you can pick up his room number."

There was a pay phone on the corner. I used it to call John Henning. I told him where we were. "Bring Vanilla, John. I'll meet you in Portsmith Square."

Portsmith Square was filled, mostly with elderly Chinese. One man in his seventies, clad in pajamas, was performing a graceful karate exercise in precise, balletlike movements under sycamore trees that looked sculpted without their leaves.

A group of pigeons reluctantly took flight into the pewter-gray sky to escape the clutches of two small Chinese schoolboys. A Catholic nun, one hand holding on to her habit to keep it from sailing away in the strong breeze, yelled to the boys in an authoritative voice and they reluctantly returned to their more orderly classmates.

"Great, huh?" I said to Vanilla Hale. "A nun with a brogue as thick as Irish soda bread shouting in Chinese to

157

a bunch of first-graders who were probably in Hong Kong a few months ago. This town does have its charms."

We were sitting on a dark-green wooden bench, directly across from the Holiday Inn. Vanilla was bundled up in a heavy coat and wool scarf. She snuggled closer to me.

"He's in there?" she said, nodding her head toward the hotel.

"Yep. Went in over an hour ago, hasn't come out since. We've got people on all the exits." I stood up. "Don't worry about a thing. I'll be right back. John and Gary will take care of you."

Henning and Gary Bartolotti were huddled a few feet behind us.

I kissed Vanilla on her cheek. "Here we go," I said, standing up and nodding to Henning and Bartolotti. "Wait ten minutes," I told Henning. "Then take her to the motel."

I crossed to the hotel and rode the elevator to the eleventh floor. Weeks's operative had been standing behind Norton when he checked in, getting the key to room 1114.

I knocked on the door.

"Come in, it's not locked," came the muffled reply.

Alan Norton was perched on the edge of a chair against the far wall. It was a typical Holiday Inn room, large bed, dresser, round table, four chairs, everything done in beige and orange. Norton was pointing an automatic pistol at me.

"Close the door behind you," Norton said, waiting until the door was closed before rising. "I'm afraid I'll have to check you out. Kindly turn around, hands on the wall. You know the drill."

I dropped the large manila folder I was carrying to

158

the floor and did as I was told. He impressed me with the gun in more ways than one. There was no way he could have had it on the plane. It must have been waiting for him in his room. He patted me down very professionally.

"All right, turn around," he said.

We circled each other warily, like dogs before a fight.

"I assume the manuscript is in that envelope," Norton said, pointing the barrel of the gun to the floor.

"That's right. Help yourself."

He bent down, keeping his eyes on me all the time, and picked the envelope up, hefting it in his left hand.

"Not very heavy," he said.

"Not all of it's there. That's just a sample. You're going to have to pay to get the rest."

"And the notes?"

"Right. And the notes."

He slipped his gun into his waistband and flopped onto the bed. "I think you're wasting my time."

"Maybe your time, but not Bledsoe's. Before you look at the pages, come over here."

I walked over to the room's window and pulled back the drapes."

"I've already seen the view. It's overrated."

"I think you'll like this. Vanilla Hale is standing between two of my men. By the bench in the park."

He pulled out his gun and waved me away from the window. He had no trouble spotting her. "She always seems to end up between two men," he said, watching my eyes for a reaction.

"Maybe she likes it that way. Anyway, I've got her now."

"So?"

"Between her, the manuscript, and those notes, I've got good old Martin Bledsoe by the balls."

"Bullshit."

"I bet old Marty was pretty short with you, Alan. You really should have found the manuscript yourself. Now, I don't want much. Just a quarter of a million dollars. That won't make too big a dent in Bledsoe's Swiss account."

Norton put his gun back in his belt and went back to the bed. He opened the envelope and went through the papers. After ten minutes he tapped them neatly on the edge of the bed and put them back in the envelope.

"Interesting" was his only comment.

"I think so. But you're just a messenger boy. I want to deal with Bledsoe. Directly. Get him out here or I start shopping those notes around to Slate's publisher. It will make a hell of a lot more interesting book that way."

Norton stood and stretched his muscles. He walked over to his suitcase and pulled out a bottle of Black Label scotch, then went to the bathroom and came back with two cellophane-covered plastic glasses.

"You'd think that they could provide real glass at these prices, wouldn't you?" he said, ripping the cellophane off and opening the whisky bottle. He poured two equal amounts into the glasses and handed me one.

He took a sip, swishing the liquor around in his mouth before swallowing it. "There's one problem about the material you're trying to sell, Polo. You'll keep copies and come back for more money."

I shook my head. "We're both professionals, Norton. The publisher already has the manuscript. The notes are a one-time shot. If the publisher puts enough people onto the project, they can probably turn up the same information Slate did. You must have samples of Slate's handwriting; check it against the papers in the manuscript. What I'm selling you is a head start. You can destroy or alter the records, so that by the time they get there, they won't find anything. Or they'll find whatever you want them to find."

Norton took another sip of his whisky. "His golf bag at the club. I should have thought of that."

"You can't think of everything," I said, putting my still-full glass down on the table. "Call Bledsoe. I want him here when we make the exchange. I'll contact you in a few hours."

21

Vanilla was dozing when I got back to the motel.

John Henning was waiting outside the door to our unit. "I'm a little worried about the lady, Nick," he said. "She's wound tighter than a drum."

"She's had a tough week, John. She's been through hell. She's probably sick and tired of being pushed around by the male race. Us included. Hang on for a few more minutes, will you?"

I went to use the pay phone near the motel parking lot, found that I didn't have any change, and had to go back and bum some quarters from Henning.

I called Jane Tobin at the *Bulletin*. She has many wonderful, charming characteristics. Subtlety is not one of them.

"Nick Polo, famous star of television and newspapers. Friends of those who have no friends. Enemy to those who have done him dozens of favors in the past, and

162

don't even get a phone call when he lands in the middle of a juicy story. Where the hell have you been?"

"Jane, I couldn't give you anything. The FBI had me tied in a knot."

"Bullshit," she said, loud enough to rattle the receiver in my hand. "You called and asked for a list of everyone who played in the Bob Hope tournament, and whose name is on that list? None other than Nicholas Theodopoulos, who just may be, and here I'm quoting from one of the reporters who did get to write a story, 'one of the biggest international murderers since Hitler.' Just don't expect any more favors, Mr. Nicholas Polo."

"Wait, wait," I yelled before she hung up. "There's more to the story. I've been saving it for you. I just need one more favor."

"How much more to the story?"

"You won't believe it, Jane. It's big."

"And just what kind of favor is it you need now?"

"I'd like you to baby-sit for me."

I went back to the room and sent Henning home. Vanilla was still asleep; she must have taken some of the pills the doctor had prescribed.

Half an hour later there was a light tapping on the door. I opened it cautiously. It was Jane Tobin. Her eyes widened when she saw Vanilla on the bed. I hushed her and walked out on the balcony with her.

"That's some baby you want me to sit with, Nick. What the hell is going on here?"

"It's all tied up with Theodopoulos, Jane. That's the woman who was in the newspapers, Vanilla Hale. She's all strung out. I have a few loose ends to tie up. She needs

163

someone to talk to, and all she's had for the last couple of days is me."

Jane smiled. "Yes, I know how much of a strain that can be," she said.

Jane is slightly over five feet tall, has auburn hair, green eyes, a peaches-and-cream complexion with just a few freckles sprinkled across her nose and cheeks. She has a knockout of a figure, which is usually disguised under her working outfit, corduroy pants, shirt, and jacket, as it was today. An oversized leather purse stuffed with tablets and pens hung over her shoulder.

"She needs company," I said. "And I need someone to look after her. It's important that she doesn't go out, or use the phone, after I've gone."

Jane pushed out both arms, like a referee calling a foul. "Hold on, Nick. I don't mind keeping someone in need company, but I'm not a bodyguard."

"Jane, she really needs help. By tomorrow I'll have her out of trouble and be handing you a hell of a story. Just stay with her for a few hours. She's too tired to be any trouble. She's just scared."

She sighed, then said, "Damn it, you always could talk me into anything." She swung her purse in the general direction of my groin. "Almost anything."

We chit-chatted on the balcony until Vanilla woke up. I introduced Jane to her. There was a noticeable chill in the air at first. I went out for sandwiches and coffee. They seemed to be getting along better when I got back with the food. The subject under their discussion was hemlines. It seemed like a serious subject to both of them. I turned on the TV and watched an old *Perry Mason* re-rerun.

Duane Weeks called an hour later. "Norton left his room, walked around Chinatown, used a public phone in a bar, then came out and gave me a wave. A one-finger wave. Then he took a cab back to the airport."

"Did he have his luggage with him?" I asked anxiously.

"No. That's where we're at now. It looks like he's waiting for someone."

Bledsoe must have been planning to fly out on a later flight all along. He couldn't be arriving at the airport now, if Norton had just called him after I left his room. There hadn't been time. *If* it was Bledsoe that Norton was planning to meet at the airport. Maybe Norton's call was just to check the arrival schedules. I covered the phone's mouthpiece and asked Vanilla, "What does Bledsoe look like?"

"Gray hair, fat, red-faced, close to sixty."

I passed the description on to Weeks. "If Norton meets someone who looks like that and they split up, forget about Norton. Keep with the fat man. Hopefully he'll be our target, Martin Bledsoe."

"You got it," Weeks said, "I'll be in touch."

I heaved a sigh of relief after Weeks's next phone call.

"They stayed together, Nick. Took a cab to the Fairmont Hotel. Martin Bledsoe registered under his own name. He matches the description perfectly."

I heaved another sigh of relief. "Good work, Duane."

"What now?" Weeks asked.

"Stick with Bledsoe, Duane. If he leaves the hotel, call me."

I tried calling Bledsoe at the Fairmont. There was no answer. Where the hell was he? Weeks said he just checked in. Probably in the bar, or getting something to eat. I tried Norton's hotel. Again no answer. Time went by slowly as I sipped cold coffee and nibbled on jagged fingernails. Either Vanilla was taking this all very calmly, or the drugs in her system were still playing havoc with her lifestyle. She dozed off again. Jane and I played a few hands of gin.

I finally made contact with Norton at the Holiday Inn.

"We deal, Mr. Polo. Just you and me. Keep those clowns you've had following me all day out of the way. This is just between us. I'll have the money. You be sure to have the necessary information. Meet me in front of my hotel at eleven."

He hung up before I could get a word in, but what the hell, I'd heard all I needed to hear.

I called the Fairmont and had Weeks paged.

"Any movement from Bledsoe?"

"Nope. Norton left about half an hour ago."

So Norton and Bledsoe had been in his room. Just not taking calls. If they were trying to make me nervous, they had succeeded. "Okay, Duane, thanks. That'll do it. Send me a bill."

"Will I ever," he said, chuckling. "I hope you've got a client to pay for all of this, Nick."

"Where to?" the cab driver asked.

"Just drive around for a while," Alan Norton said as he and I clambered into the back of the taxi.

The driver pulled into the heavy traffic on Kearny Street. I caught his eyes as he looked into the rear-view mirror. We must have been quite a sight. Two guys patting themselves all over the place. He was probably used to it; two closet gays checking out their ward-robes.

"Satisfied?" asked Alan Norton, handing me his rain-coat.

"Not quite. Your belt. As I remember, the buckle's quite sharp."

He upturned both palms and smiled. "I knew you'd remember, so I didn't bother wearing it."

"You don't mind if I check, do you?"

The driver's eyes went back to his mirror as I undid Norton's belt. The buckle seemed normal.

"So," Norton said, "now we're both reasonably sure we're both unarmed, and if one of us is wearing a bug, it's in such an uncomfortable spot it's not worth looking for." He looked out the cab's back window, then told the driver, "Make some right turns."

"Right turns, what the—"

"Just do it," Norton commanded.

The driver shifted uneasily in his seat. Norton kept his eyes on the traffic behind us.

"Quit worrying," I said. "There's no one back there. It's just between you and me."

"What have you told Vanilla about our negotiations?"

"Not much. She's got enough problems."

Norton arched an eyebrow. "Oh?"

"Seems to be having a relapse. Must have taken the wrong medicine," I said.

"How unfortunate." He must have been convinced we weren't being followed. He turned to the driver. "Take us to the Golden Gate bridge," he said, his hands moving nervously along the small leather briefcase in his lap. There should be two hundred and fifty thousand dollars in the case.

We cruised past the Marina Green and onto the bridge approach.

"Where to now?" asked the driver.

"Just keep driving," Norton said.

The only noise was the zip of the tires on the road. Norton started peeking over his shoulder again. When we were almost across the bridge he said, "Pull in at Vista Point."

The cab came to a halt in the parking lot at the northeast end of the bridge.

Norton paid off the driver. There were twenty or more cars in the lot. He stalked off back toward the bridge and I followed. The fog was thick and my rubber-soled shoes were making kissing sounds on the damp walkway. "You picked a nice spot," I told Norton.

"This bridge always disappointed me. It's not golden at all."

"International orange," I said over the noise of a large truck rumbling by. Traffic was very light, and though I couldn't see more than twenty-five yards in any direction, there were no signs of any other pedestrians. Norton had picked well. No one in his right mind would be walking across the bridge at this time of the night.

"Since we're almost partners now," I said, "tell me something. Did you ever figure out just how Slate and Dykstra tied Theodopoulos into being Zadar?"

"That dumb camel jockey," Norton said contemptuously. "He wasn't satisfied. Spent a bloody fortune on plastic surgery, hair transplants, even tried having his fingerprints burned off. He was terrified of being found out at first. Then he got a taste of the good life, wanted to hang around with the rich and famous, movie stars, professional athletes. Started entering those golf tournaments where the wealthy amateurs pay thousands just to play with some plaid-pants professionals. Dykstra was guarding Gerald Ford in Palm Springs a couple of weeks ago. One of Ford's bloody golf balls went off course, hit some dumb bastard in the head. Zadar was there. He laughed. As only

168

that asshole could laugh. He said Dykstra looked right at him. He knew right then that Dykstra knew it was him. Dykstra had been to Iran, with Henry Kissinger, on one of his famous shuttle diplomacy trips during the Nixon years. Zadar had given Dykstra the Cook's Tour of their interrogation room. Apparently some of Zadar's men were literally skinning some poor beggar alive. Dykstra lost his lunch and ran from the room. Zadar had laughed at him, said he called him a 'typical gutless American.'"

I remembered Zadar's laugh at the banquet. It was unique, all right. "You mean to tell me that Dykstra pegged him just from that one laugh?"

"Apparently. Zadar said he saw Dykstra following him around, taking photographs. He heard he was asking questions about him. Then he saw Dykstra and Slate together. He knew about Slate's upcoming book. That's all the information the dumb sand nigger needed."

He waved the case in his hand. "The money's in here."

We walked by the north tower and out around the observation platform. I leaned against the massive girder. We were protected now, both from the chilling wind and from the view of any passing motorists.

I took an envelope from my jacket pocket and handed it to Norton. "Here's all the notes on the bank accounts and the rest of the manuscript. Mind if I take a look at that money?"

He snatched the envelope angrily and handed me the case. I unlatched the locks and let a couple of packets of bills fall to the ground.

"Shit," I yelled, "there goes the money."

Norton stooped down for a minisecond, his left hand reaching for the bills, which were now blowing close to the bridge's railing. It was all the time I'd ever get. I

169

lashed out with a foot, catching him squarely in the kneecap, then brought the edge of the briefcase across his face, the brass fittings slashing into his nose. He fell back against the railing, and I kicked at him again. I had a feeling that Norton would be a millionth-degree black belt in all those weird kung fu, tai chi, karate-judo techniques, so if I didn't hurt him quick, I was a dead man. Although he had the build of a man who worked out regularly in a gym, I felt that I would have him beat in the strength department. I had spent my early youth working for my father as a hod carrier and two long summers as a deckhand on one of those picturesque little fishing boats you see tied up at Fisherman's Wharf. Hauling up crab pots and fishnets gives you the kind of muscle power that stays with you all your life. Norton started blocking blows with his forearms, but I caught him with one more good kick in the groin, then an elbow square on the face. His nose opened like an overripe watermelon. He fell to the ground and I hauled him up quickly, hoisting him headfirst over the railing, his feet tucked under my arms.

He tried kicking back, but his strength was gone. Blood was streaming out of his mouth and nose, making speech difficult.

"Let me up," he screamed, his hands searching desperately for a hold on the bridge's slippery steel.

I let him slip down a few more inches. "No telling how much longer I can hold onto you, Alan. So talk. Where's Bledsoe now?"

He used a hand to try and stem the flow of blood from his nose. "His room at the Fairmont. Number nineteen thirty-eight. He's waiting there for me."

"Who's with him?"

"No one. He's alone."

I opened my arms and he slid down a few more inches.

"I'm not lying. He's alone, damn it."

"My back's killing me, Alan. I figure I can hold onto you about another minute or so. Tell me the plan. Were you going to kill both me and Vanilla?"

"No, no," he screamed, panic in his voice.

"Don't lie to me, Alan. You killed Zadar because he was a loose cannon. You wouldn't let Vanilla and me walk around with what we know."

"All right. Bledsoe wanted you killed, not the girl. But I can talk to him, make him understand."

"Who killed Slate and Dykstra?"

"That dumb fucker, Zadar. It wasn't us. It was him. He was crazy."

"What about Paul Sanders?" I asked, letting him slip down another inch.

"Who? I don't know . . ."

"The private investigator in Monterey, Alan. You better start answering a little faster. I'm tiring quickly."

"Sanders, yes, Sanders, he was a fool. I met him at his house. He took a swing at me, said he was going to turn me over to the police, I—"

"Okay, forget Sanders. Just what was the deal between Zadar and Bledsoe?"

"Money. What else? Zadar had access to some of the shah's money and knew where a lot more was. He needed help to get to it. Bledsoe helped him, that's all. Helped him get the money, and helped him get a new identity."

"What about Dykstra's wife? Did you kill her?"

"It was an accident. Zadar had tapped Slate's phone. He overheard a conversation Dykstra had with Slate. Dykstra was getting ready to retire. He had started a book of his own. I went down to check the house. She was supposed to be out all afternoon, but she walked in unexpectedly. I had to—"

"Two hundred and forty feet down to the water,

171

Alan. Try not to go in feet first, or the coroner will find you wearing your balls for earrings."

He screamed again, his hands desperately grabbing at the fog-slick railings, gaining a hold momentarily, then being pulled free by the weight of his body as he cartwheeled down toward the icy bay waters.

22

"Don't do anything foolish, son," Martin Bledsoe said, backing away from the door into his hotel room. Room actually didn't do justice to the place. It was a suite. A large suite. The floor was covered by a thick Persian rug. The walls were done in flocked wallpaper, the furniture all white with gold accents.

Bledsoe was pretty much as Vanilla had described him: gray hair, fat, red-faced, on either side of sixty. But he was an impressive, graying, fat, red-faced man. The hair was thin, but expensively barbered. The fat well clothed in dark-blue pajamas under a red-and-black checked silk robe. The red in his face looked like it got there from very old Burgundies, not jug wine. He projected the image of what he was: a wealthy, powerful prick. A half-smoked, thick black cigar with over an inch of ash nestled between the pudgy fingers of his right hand.

173

He pulled his robe tightly around his protruding stomach and settled himself into a caneback regal chair with as much dignity as he could muster.

"I take it I won't be seeing Alan tonight?" he said.

"Not unless you feel like swimming in very cold water," I said, peeking around the rest of the room.

There was a bottle of Glenlivet whisky standing alongside a Lucite ice bucket on a table near the window. The neck of an opened bottle of champagne protruded from the ice bucket. There were two glasses on the table, one a short highball glass with some of the scotch in it, the other a tall, thin flute with champagne bubbling up from the bottom. There was a lipstick smudge on the champagne glass.

"I hope I'm not breaking up a party," I said.

"Not at all, sir, not at all," Bledsoe said.

I topped off his scotch glass and carried it over to him. "Maybe you better tell your friend to leave," I said, handing him the glass.

"Actually, she's a friend of both of ours, Mr. Polo. I assume you are Mr. Polo."

"You assume correctly. I think we should talk business, Bledsoe, and—"

"Hi, Nick," Vanilla Hale said, as she came into the room from a door against the far wall.

She was wearing a red velvet V-necked dress with long sleeves, slashed down far enough to show there were no undergarments needed with this outfit. A diamond necklace sparkled on her neck. Matching diamond earrings showed from under her hair. I was stunned, and for some reason the first question that came to my mind was Where the hell did she get the dress? Good old Martin must have felt confident enough to bring it along for her, or more likely the hotel's boutique had it in stock.

I marched over and grabbed Bledsoe by the neck. "Where's Jane Tobin?" I shouted at Vanilla.

"Please, please, Mr. Polo," Bledsoe said, trying to wiggle away from my grasp. "Your friend is fine. Vanilla came here of her own free will. If she wants to leave with you now, that's also her choice."

I kept my hand on his neck. "Who else have you got hiding in the other room?"

"Not a soul, I assure you. Go and check while I fix you a drink, sir. We have much to discuss."

I let go of his neck and grabbed the small finger of his left hand in a come-along hold and pulled him from the chair. He protested until I tightened the tension on his finger, then he got up, and I dragged him into the other room, which was a large bedroom. The bedspread was covered with dresses, blues, reds, blacks, all expensive looking, all in styles that looked like they would do justice to Vanilla's curves. I checked the bathroom and the closets before letting go of Bledsoe's pinky.

"That was all quite unnecessary," he said, shaking the pain from his finger and turning on his slippered feet and marching back to the other room. He found another glass and poured me a large slug of the scotch.

"Your good health, sir," he said, raising his glass to me, tilting his head and taking an audible sip. "And if you happen to have a tape recorder or microphone concealed on your person, Mr. Polo, believe me, it will serve you no purpose."

You could tell he must have a lot of conversations with attorneys. I scanned the room again but didn't see what I was looking for: ultrasonic microphone jammers.

Small, innocent-looking boxes that emit constantly changing ultrasonic signals that a tape recorder or bug mike picks up along with the room's audio, making anything recorded just a jumble of incoherent sounds. They're all the vogue now. About the first thing corporate America decorates their offices with is a shredder and a microphone jammer. I was sure Bledsoe would have plenty of them sprinkled around the suite, you need at least four to cover a room thoroughly.

Vanilla just stood there, her eyes vacant, her mouth slightly open.

"Your man Alan wasn't thinking much of my health a little while ago," I said. The phone was one of those fancy French models, all ivory and gold. I called the motel first. There was no answer. I then called Jane Tobin's home number. She answered on the first ring.

"Are you all right?" I asked.

"Yes, I'm fine, Nick, she just took off and I—"

"No one has bothered you?"

"No, no one, she just—"

"Okay, I'm at the Fairmont, room nineteen thirty-eight. If I don't call you back in half an hour, call the police."

I hung up and took a long sip of the scotch. "You certainly are full of surprises, Vanilla," I said.

She shrugged those elegant shoulders. "Nick, I'm sorry for all the trouble I put you through, but I just knew that Martin hadn't meant for all this to happen. I just had to talk to him."

"Him and his jeweler and his wardrobe mistress, I guess."

Bledsoe sat down in the caneback chair. He leaned back until it creaked, like elderly, arthritic joints.

"Please, Mr. Polo. Sit down. Finish your drink. We've got to talk."

"Fuck you, Bledsoe." Not very polished or witty, but it certainly described my feelings better than anything else I could think of saying.

"Mr. Polo. We are both businessmen. Surely we can discuss this in a rational manner. There's been too much unnecessary violence already."

"Unnecessary violence? I guess you could call it that. But what do you consider necessary violence? Killing a Secret Service agent's wife? Setting up Vanilla as a sexual football for Theodopoulos, or Zadar, or whatever the hell his name was? Trying to have me killed twice? Unnecessary violence. What a polite term for murder."

He held up both hands like a boxer warding off blows. "Please, that was not my doing. This man you know as Alan, that was his doing. He was never authorized to do any of that, believe me."

"He was your man."

Bledsoe flashed a smile that must have been dynamite at a board meeting. All the teeth and parts of his gums were gleaming at me. "Theoretically, I guess you could assume that, sir. But if push came to shove, I assure you that there would be no possible way to tie that man's employment to me in any way."

I looked at Vanilla. She pulled her eyes away and walked over and poured herself some champagne.

"Where does all this leave us, Bledsoe?" I said.

"You got what you wanted, Mr. Polo. The money. You should be happy. Vanilla is happy. Why don't we just shake hands and go our own ways?"

"I'm afraid that there's not much of the money left. Most of it was literally blown away. Gone with the wind."

Bledsoe was listening with his eyes almost shut. He

wrapped his thick lips around his cigar, inhaled deeply, and let out a long cloud of smoke.

"I supplied the agreed amount of money," he said. "What happened to it in delivery cannot be blamed on me. My instructions were to hand it over to you, straight and simple. So if you are looking for more money, I'm afraid you'll have to look somewhere else."

"When Alan went swimming, he didn't have the rest of the manuscript and the notes, Bledsoe."

His eyes popped open. "So you want to sell them to me. Again."

"No. I want to give them away. To the FBI. The police, Slate's publisher, the newspapers. Anyone who can use them."

Bledsoe's voice hardened. "That would be a mistake, sir. A terrible mistake."

"Why? What are you going to do, Bledsoe? Kill me? Enough people will know about my connection to the notes to make that dangerous for you."

He smiled, then laughed, softly at first, then deeper, his belly bouncing up and down. He set his drink on the floor and wiped his eyes with his hands. "My God," he finally said. "It was a bluff, wasn't it? All a bluff. You really don't have anything, do you? Nothing worth the price of a drink, much less a quarter of a million dollars." He started laughing again. "Yes, very good, sir. Very good indeed." He reached back down for his drink and raised it in a toast to me. "Well done."

I turned to Vanilla. She was holding her champagne glass in one hand, her hip resting against a dresser. "What about you, Vanilla? Going back to Washington with your pimp? Back to the good life? Maybe he can set you up with someone new. Someone else who's trying to get the goods on him. Maybe the new man will be younger, better looking than Slate. More of a jet-setter. More in your league."

She just stared back at me with vacant eyes. "I . . . I'm sorry, Nick," she finally said. "Really sorry."

It wasn't until I was in the elevator that I came up with the line I should have used: with wrinkled forehead and squinting eyes. "Frankly, my dear, I just don't give a damn."

23

"What do you feel like doing about it, Nick?" Jane Tobin asked.

"Jumping off the bridge, but I don't think I'd like the company down below."

We were in Jane's apartment. I had told her the whole story. She had started taking notes but stopped about halfway through.

"You're going to have to go to the police."

"I will. I'll meet with Shroyer tomorrow, but what the hell is he going to do? I can't tell him about Alan Norton going over the side of the Golden Gate bridge. I can't show him those bank accounts, because I got them illegally. Shroyer isn't exactly in love with me now. If he could pin something, anything, on me, he'd do it with pleasure."

Jane went to the kitchen and came back with the coffeepot and a bottle of amaretto. She refilled my cup and sprinkled a dash of the liqueur on top.

"Couldn't the FBI get the bank information?"

"Sure. Eventually. But by the time they did, Bledsoe would have the money transferred and buried. He was right. I really didn't have anything. It was all a bluff."

Jane plopped down on the couch alongside me. "Vanilla, she really got to you, didn't she?"

"A little," I admitted. "I set her up with that stupid phone call at the restaurant. Maybe if I didn't have John Henning make that call, she never would have ended up at Zadar's place."

"Don't feel sorry for her. She can handle herself. Did I tell you how she got away from me at the motel?"

I sipped at the coffee. "No."

"She said she was hungry, so I called out and ordered a pizza. When the delivery boy got there, she gave him a big smile, a twenty-dollar bill, and asked if he would mind escorting her outside, that I was 'bothering her.' What could I do, Nick?"

"Nothing, Jane. Nothing."

"What do you think will happen? To Vanilla and Bledsoe, I mean?" she said.

"From what I know of Bledsoe, he won't keep her around long. He'll find another Alan Norton somewhere to do his heavy work. All I've done is make things unpleasant for him for a little while. I probably actually did the bastard a favor by exposing Theodopoulos as Zadar. Zadar must have been a continuing pain in the ass to Bledsoe."

She leaned over and ran a hand through my hair.

"You look so sad," she said, kissing my ear. "Isn't there anything we can do to cheer you up?"

I smiled into those beautiful green eyes. "How about a pizza?"

181